Return from Witch Mountain

Also by Martin Mellett
Warrior Queen

Return from Witch Mountain

by Martin Mellett

Based on Walt Disney Productions'
motion picture screenplay
written by

Malcolm Marmorstein

Based on characters created by

Alexander Key

Scholastic Publications
in association with Pan Books

Published in Great Britain 1979 by Pan Books Ltd,
Cavaye Place, London SW10 9PG
This edition published 1979 by Scholastic Publications Ltd,
in association with Pan Books Ltd
© Walt Disney Productions 1978
ISBN 0 330 25754 4
Printed and bound in Great Britain by
Cox & Wyman Ltd, London, Reading and Fakenham

Contents

1	The Visit	7
2	The Earthquakes	21
3	The Experiment	34
4	The Plan	43
5	The Heist	52
6	The Chase	62
7	The Trap	71
8	The Rescue	83
9	The Countdown	94
10	The Duel	101

1 The Visit

The strange, unearthly whine pierced the stillness of the blue morning sky. From behind the tall grey mountains in the east, a shimmering silver disc rose gracefully into the air and, dropping to a low altitude, raced effortlessly across the flat open countryside. It streaked along at a breath-taking rate and, as it drew near the city, a flashing band of light showed clearly around its rim. The eerie high-pitched noise gradually grew louder until, as the shining craft approached the huge oval Rose Bowl football stadium, it began to cut its speed.

With motors winding down, the gleaming saucer came to a halt above the deserted stadium, hovering directly over the centre of the field. It remained suspended there for a few seconds, like a mysterious chandelier hanging inside some great glass-roofed hall. Then slowly, gently, it began to descend in a perfectly straight line to within a few feet of the ground. Suddenly, a wide beam of light shot from beneath the craft and three figures materialized inside it. They were softly transported to the short grass of the football field.

At first, the dazzling ray concealed its cargo from view, but as they stepped from the beam, it became clear that the figures were human. There was a girl, a boy and a man. The youngsters were each carrying light suitcases and, as they moved away from the landing-point, they looked with interest around the stadium.

'Nice landing, Uncle Bené,' complimented the girl, whose name was Tia.

'You should have gone for a touchdown,' joked her brother, Tony.

The wide, bearded face of the youngsters' uncle split into a grin. 'Next time I'll put it right between the goalposts,' he said. Then, motioning with his big hands, he ushered his two charges towards the edge of the field. Tia, twelve years old and two years younger than her brother, was an attractive girl with an open, intelligent face, a fine spray of freckles and long flaxen hair which fell almost to her waist. She wore a smart red suit, made up of a jacket, waistcoat and culottes. Her clear, bright eyes betrayed a lively sense of humour, tempered by a sound level-headedness. In contrast, Tony had a more impish look about him: fresh-faced, with an upturned nose and longish brown hair. His casual trousers and short zipper jacket reflected a more impulsive nature than his sister.

As the group passed from the field, they found their way through one of the aisles that led between the stands and entered one of the concrete passages that would eventually bring them to the main gates. The deserted corridors echoed to the sound of their foot-steps.

'I can't wait to see the museums and go to the concerts,' said Tia.

Uncle Bené nodded and smiled to himself. He knew that this trip for Tia and Tony was long overdue, and that they both stood to benefit greatly from it. Everyone had been so busy establishing the community on Witch Mountain that neither of the young-sters had had the opportunity to see what life in a big city was all about. Which was why this brief educational visit had finally been arranged for them. Tony, however, was concerned that their excursion might turn out to be somewhat dull. Museums and concerts were a little *too* educational for his liking. 'I'd rather go to the beach and learn how to surf,' he said wryly. (He had no way of knowing that the next few days were to produce more excitement than even he could handle.)

Before either of his companions could muster a reply, the trio found themselves at the main gates. In front of them stood two high, tubular-steel and wire barriers held tightly in place by a huge padlock. Uncle Bené reached out to test them.

'Locked,' observed Tony, matter-of-factly. 'Come on.'

But Tony made no effort to move. Save that is, for the effort needed to furrow his brow in a moment's concentration. What followed after that was startling enough to have sent any innocent onlooker rushing to see a psychiatrist. Exactly as if he had stepped into an invisible elevator, the young boy from Witch Mountain began to rise slowly – and quite deliberately – into the air, suitcase in hand. Amazingly, neither Tia nor her uncle appeared to show the least surprise. Rather, Uncle Bené seemed somewhat annoyed. As Tony's feet reached the level of the top of the gate, his uncle called sharply to him, 'Tony ... come back here!'

Hovering in space, Tony looked down. 'What is it?' he asked, puzzled.

'All the way back,' ordered Uncle Bené.

Tony shrugged. With as little fuss as he had gone up, he came down again.

'You mustn't do things like that,' said Uncle Bené sternly.

'Why not?'

'Because you might frighten someone. Earth people don't understand about energizing matter.'

'We are supposed to be ordinary Earth kids,' Tia reminded her brother.

'Don't energize unless absolutely necessary,' advised Uncle Bené.

'But it *is* necessary,' argued Tony. 'The gates are locked.'

Uncle Bené shook his head. 'Tia . . .?' he said inquiringly, turning to his young niece.

Tia thought for a moment and then, closing her eyes, put her extraordinary power to work. Immediately, the big rusty padlock began to creak open, and in no time at all the huge double gates were swinging back to allow the party through. Once they were on the outside, Tia re-energized the lock and everything swung back neatly into position, exactly as it was before. Uncle Bené looked a little happier. True, Tia had utilized the same energizing powers as her brother, but her method had been a far less obvious one. Perhaps, he thought, with practice, the children could learn to live for a while without recourse to their unusual gifts. After all, Earth people enjoyed no such advantages. Putting an arm around each of the youngsters' shoulders, he guided them in the direction of the stadium's parking lot.

On the far side of the empty lot, shining bright as a pin in the morning sunshine, stood a yellow cab, with its motor ticking over. Next to it was the driver. He was pacing irritably up and down, stopping occasionally to check his watch or brush a speck of dust from his immaculate vehicle. He seemed more like a racing driver than a cabbie, dressed as he was in a colourful jumpsuit covered with a variety of sewn-on patches. One oblong patch across his left chest pocket had the name Eddie written on it. On sighting the three figures emerging from the stadium, he hopped into his taxi and slammed the gear lever into reverse. There was a piercing squeal as he jabbed the accelerator and, with tyres sending up frantic smoke signals, the car leapt backwards across the lot.

Tia, Tony and Uncle Bené side-stepped just in time as the cab pulled to a screeching halt beside them. Eddie poked his crag-like face out of the window. 'You the party what I'm supposed to pick up?' The words came in a snappy, excited gabble.

'Just the children,' explained Uncle Bené.

Eddie jumped out of the cab, opened up the rear door and snatched the luggage from Tia and Tony. 'Meter's runnin'. Hop in, hop in, hop in!'

As the children moved to comply, Eddie stepped quickly round to deposit the suitcases in the trunk. 'I been waitin' here for ever,' he fussed. 'People are supposed to wait for taxis ... not taxis for people.'

'We are exactly on time,' corrected Uncle Bené.

'Kind of strange time and place to be makin' a pickup. I mean ... if you're here for the next game, it's in three months.'

'We have seats on the fifty-yard line,' answered Uncle Bené, with a conspiratorial wink at Tia and Tony.

Eddie slammed the trunk closed and studied the bearded stranger for a moment. There was something unusual about this man, but he could not decide quite what it was. He shrugged, got back in to the car and gunned the engine. Uncle Bené leant down to hand him a slip of paper. 'Take the children to this address,' he instructed. 'You'll be paid when you arrive.'

Eddie gave a querulous look. 'This is a big fare,' he said warily. 'If them kids is gonna pay me, I hope they know I get a big tip.'

Uncle Bené moved to the back window. 'Everything has been worked out for you,' he explained to the youngsters. 'Stick to the schedule, remember what I told you, and have a wonderful time. I'll see you Friday.' They exchanged goodbyes and Uncle Bené stepped back. He was just in time. The pitch of the cab's engine changed from a growl to a dull roar as Eddie stabbed the accelerator and the vehicle shot off towards the edge of the parking lot, leaving a smell of scorched rubber in its wake. Uncle Bené had a brief glimpse of a pair of waving hands through the rear window and then the cab was gone, zooming off along the main highway towards the city.

The two youngsters sat back to enjoy the sights. This was going to be a great experience for them – five whole days to be spent exploring and learning about life in a big, exciting Earth city. Even Tony was secretly enthralled by the idea. The journey to the city flashed by. In no time at all, the cab found itself weaving a path through the mid-morning traffic that was clogging the city streets. Eddie drove as if his life depended on it – accelerating into narrow gaps, braking hard, doing racing starts away from the traffic lights. Any vehicle that got in the way was treated to a string of insults. 'Look at that dummy!' Eddie sounded a long blast on his horn as he all but forced an innocent-looking Volkswagen to mount the sidewalk. 'Get outta the way, you dummy.' He shook his head in despair. 'These civilians don't know how to drive. They oughtta be kept off the streets. The streets belong to us professional drivers. Taxis, buses and trucks ... that's all that should be on the streets. I know all there is to know about drivin'. I have a perfect safety record.' He leant on the horn again as a lone pedestrian was foolish enough to try crossing the

12

street at the intersection. 'Get off the road, you bum!' shouted Eddie, head out of the window.

Behind him, Tia and Tony laughed heartily. Their vacation was certainly getting off to a racing start.

Not more than a few blocks away, another car was gliding to a halt in a deserted side street – a car which was destined to have a far greater effect on the lives of Tia and Tony than the one in which they were now travelling. This vehicle was a sleek black Citroën DS, with dark tinted windows. As it came to a stop by the kerb, the driver's door clicked open and a tall, angular-faced man with a pock-marked complexion emerged. He moved round to the other side of the car and opened the passenger door. A woman stepped out. She was in her mid-sixties, distinctly aristocratic in appearance, with lined, eagle-like features and penetrating eyes. Her clothes were dark and sombre and somewhat dated. Her name was Letha Wedge.

'Thank you Sickle,' she said in a clipped, cultured voice. But although her tone was imperious, there was something uncomfortable in her manner as she looked up and down the street.

Meanwhile, Sickle had moved behind her and opened the rear door. Doctor Victor Gannon, a tall, severe-looking man of around fifty, got out. He was wearing a neat, business-like suit and was carrying some sort of compact electronic device in his right hand. His dark eyes were scanning a high building on the opposite side of the street.

'Looks like a perfect test site,' observed Letha.

'It's adequate,' said Gannon impassively.

Sickle shifted uneasily. 'Let's get it over with,' he prompted. Then, brushing back the hair from his right ear, he asked, 'Is this thing on okay?'

Gannon bent forward to inspect the tiny electronic receptor unit which was located there. 'It's ready,' he confirmed.

'What do you want him to do this time?' inquired Letha.

Gannon pointed to the tall red-brick building – clearly disused – on the corner of the street. 'Climb that fire escape to the absolute top,' he explained. Sickle raised his hands apprehensively. 'Hey, wait a minute,' he protested. 'This is as high as I go. You want me to break somebody's leg ... just tell me how many pieces. But don't ask me to climb up there.'

'Why not?' asked Gannon.

'Because I'm afraid of heights. I'll get dizzy and ... fall.'

'It's true, Victor,' interjected Letha. 'He has acrophobia, among other things. Find a different test for him.'

Victor Gannon allowed himself the ghost of a smile. He knew that acrophobia wasn't going to be a problem with his device. Sickle, however, was by no means convinced. He began to back slowly away. 'I'll do anything else you say, doctor ... but I won't do that!'

Calmly, with an air of complete confidence, Gannon flicked a switch on his electronic control unit. Instantly, Sickle stopped dead in his tracks. He snapped rigidly upright, a strange, vacant stare entering his eyes. He seemed like a man who had been hypnotized in the space of a split-second. Gannon raised the control unit to his mouth and spoke into it in a slow, commanding tone. 'Sickle: I order you to climb that fire escape. When you reach the top you will turn and look down. You will not be affected by the height. Now go.'

With deliberate, almost mechanical movements,

14

Sickle turned and headed across the street walking towards the fire escape.

'It's working!' exclaimed Gannon triumphantly. 'It's working!'

'So it seems,' said Letha. 'But you're risking his life. He's my nephew, my only living relative, the only one I can leave my bankruptcy to.' Gannon scowled. To him, the experiment was all that mattered. He held up the control unit as though it were a precious jewel. 'Can't you see I'm in complete control of his mind?' he gloated. 'He can only carry out my commands. I've done it!'

By this time, Sickle had reached the fire escape and had begun his long climb up the side of the high building. Gannon looked on with the glint of success in his eyes – but Letha Wedge could not bring herself to share his enthusiasm.

Meanwhile, Eddie the cab driver had run into a different kind of problem. Turning left off the main street in order to take a short cut across town, he had put his foot down hard, trying to beat a set of traffic lights at the next intersection. That was when his engine had started to splutter and cut out. An expression of pure disbelief came across his face. After all, how could there possibly be anything wrong with a vehicle driven and serviced by the world's finest cab driver?

In the back seat, Tony was already concentrating on the problem. Probing the car's engine with his amazing mental powers, he soon came up with the answer. 'Out of gas,' he reported.

'What, are you – crazy?' retorted Eddie. 'Look at the gas gauge. It points to ... to ...' His face fell. The tell-tale needle clearly indicated an empty tank. With the engine starved of fuel, the cab coasted silently to a stop by the kerb. Eddie groaned and slapped the steering wheel. Jumping out, he dashed round to the trunk and extracted an empty gas can. Then he popped his head into the rear window. 'It was all that waitin' I hadda do for you. Now I'll hafta run down the street to the gas station. You're costin' me a lotta dough. You better make the tip worth it.' Before Tia or Tony could reply, he was speeding off down the street, gas can swinging wildly at his side.

The youngsters smiled at each other and settled back for the wait. But suddenly, without warning, both their faces creased into deep frowns. Both of them reached a hand towards their foreheads. Their super-sensitive minds had simultaneously been afflicted by the same sense of impending danger. They had both been given a fleeting mental glimpse of a frightening image – a hazy vision of a figure falling helplessly through space. It was impossible to make out more, as the image disappeared as suddenly as it had come. Tia looked into her brother's eyes. Each knew the other had seen it. There was a questioning look in Tia's eyes.

Tony shook his head slowly. Finally, he said, 'Something's going to happen to someone ... near here ...' His sister nodded. They both knew that their premonition might concern a matter of life and death. Tia touched her brother's arm. 'Let's try to help,' she ventured. Tony thought for a moment. 'You'd better wait for the driver,' he suggested, 'I'll go.' Before his sister had a chance to argue, he had the car door open and was stepping on to the sidewalk.

He glanced quickly up and down the street, trying to orientate himself. 'I think it came from that direction,' he concluded, indicating a side turning about a hundred yards along the street. Tia had her head out of the window. 'Hurry back,' she said anxiously. 'And remember what Uncle Bené said.'

Tony smiled tersely and, raising a hand in agreement, hurried off down the street. A moment later he had disappeared around the corner.

Letha was looking more agitated than ever. Sickle had arrived at the top of the fire escape and was now balanced precariously on the ledge, staring vacantly into space. A dozen storeys below, Letha tugged at Gannon's sleeve, imploring him to bring Sickle down but Gannon brushed her away. He had come out to test his mind-control device to the full – and he would not be satisfied with anything less. He addressed himself to the control unit. 'Sickle,' he said slowly, 'turn to the right ... balance yourself ... and walk along the ledge ... now!'

'No!' pleaded Letha. But her protests were to no avail. Like some obedient zombie, Sickle turned and proceeded along the narrow ledge, oblivious to the dizzying height.

'Stop him!' cried Letha.

'I won't stop in the middle of a test,' insisted Gannon, who was too intoxicated with his achievement to heed Letha's pleas. 'I can make him do anything!' he gloated. 'I'm in complete control ...'

In desperation, Letha made a wild grab for the control unit. If she succeeded in snatching it away from Gannon, she could bring Sickle down herself. But the doctor held on tightly to the device and a fierce struggle developed. It seemed for a moment as if Letha might wrest it from him, but then the unit slid from both their grasps and went flying through the air. It hit the ground in a shower of sparks and a series of protesting bleeps. There was a puff of blue smoke and then silence. High up on the roof, Sickle twitched involuntarily and teetered dangerously on the edge. Then he straightened up again and continued along the ledge as though nothing had happened.

Gannon's face was a mask of fury as he scrambled to pick up his control unit. Frenziedly, he began punching out a sequence of buttons. 'Look what you've done!' he yelled. 'Sickle ... Sickle, stop!' He thumped the device. 'I command you to stop!'

But the human guinea-pig was not responding. Slowly, deliberately, he was approaching the open end of the ledge. 'He's out of control!' cried Gannon, his voice a mixture of frustration and panic.

'Sickle! go back!' screamed Letha.

Unheeding, Sickle walked on. The corner of the ledge drew nearer. Twenty feet, fifteen feet, ten ...

Just around the corner of the street, Tony paused in his stride as his sister's telepathic voice reached out to him across three blocks. *'Tony ... have you found it?'* came the anxious question.

Tony closed his eyes. *'Not yet,'* he replied, *'but I'm close, very close ...'* Then he rounded the corner and everything seemed to happen at once. The hapless Sickle had reached the point of no return. Without the slightest hesitation in his stride, he stepped straight off into space. Letha squealed and turned quickly away, covering her eyes. Gannon looked on in horror as Sickle plunged silently earthward, like a lifeless manikin.

Tony grasped the situation in a flash and reacted with lightning speed. Instinctively, his energizing powers reached out to save the falling man. Sickle suddenly came to a halt, as if he had hit a huge invisible pillow. He had been de-gravitated, scant feet from the sidewalk and was hanging in mid-air, still completely unaware what was happening to him. Gannon's mouth dropped open. 'Letha ... look!' he exclaimed.

'I can't,' she replied fearfully.

'You've got to! Tell me I'm seeing what I'm seeing!' Gannon grabbed her harshly and spun her around. For a moment she was speechless. She looked as if she had been struck by a thunderbolt. Eventually, she said. 'Is your control unit having some sort of side-effect?'

'It's not my control. It's that ... that boy.' Gannon pointed incredulously to Tony, who was standing on the opposite corner of the street. As he and Letha watched, they saw Tony gently energize Sickle and transport him the remaining few feet to the ground, reaching out to balance him and set him upright.

'It's miraculous!' enthused Letha.

'There are no miracles,' scoffed Gannon. 'Only scientific answers for everything.'

'Then explain what we've just seen.'

Gannon thought for moment, trying to apply his academic brain to the mystifying events he had just witnessed. 'We've seen a force ...' he mused, 'a force which counteracts the basic law of gravity.'

'Victor ... I don't know what you're saying.'

'I know exactly what I'm saying – and seeing! Molecular mobilization!' Gannon thumped a fist into an open palm. A cruel cold glint flashed briefly in his eye. His voice grew much quieter and when he next spoke, an edge of determination had crept into it. 'I need that boy,' he said evenly. 'I need him desperately!'

Letha nodded. She still wasn't quite sure what Gannon was talking about, but somehow she could sense that her partner's scientific mind was on the right track. Together, they started across the street towards their quarry.

When they got there, they found Tony trying to console the disorientated Sickle. He wasn't having much success. Gannon waved his arms enthusiastically as he approached. 'Brilliant! brilliant!' he beamed. He took Sickle firmly in hand and moved him to a position against the wall of the building, just behind Tony who had turned to face the oncoming Letha.

'Young man,' said Letha in an overbearing, phoney sort of way. 'Congratulations on a fantastic ... er ... whatever it was you did. It was absolutely heroic!' Her rouged lips parted in a huge smile. 'You deserve a reward.' She began to rummage in her purse for some money. Tony started to decline the offer. 'I don't want any ...' he began but suddenly could not think of the words he needed to complete the sentence. Instead, he felt a sharp pain in his right arm. He found himself opening his eyes very wide, and then shutting them very quickly. He could not understand what was making him do that, nor what caused him, a second later, to topple forward into Letha's outstretched arms. But after that, the problem ceased to matter.

Behind him, Doctor Victor Gannon stood with a self-satisfied smirk on his face and a hypodermic needle in his right hand.

2 The Earthquakes

Three blocks away, Tia winced in pain and clutched her right arm. She knew that something terrible had happened. She had been 'tuned in' to Tony's mental wavelength and now, much like a blip disappearing from a radar screen, it had gone completely dead. Frantically, she transmitted her thoughts in an effort to re-establish contact. *'Tony ... what happened?'* she called. *'Where are you? Tony!'*

But there was no reply. Tia's heartbeat quickened. Her brother must be in trouble – bad trouble. He would need her help. She scrambled hurriedly out of the taxi and raced off down the street, following the path Tony had taken only a few minutes earlier. Her sole thought was to find him again, as quickly as possible.

Tia ran very fast, and her uncanny sense of direction took her to the exact location of Tony's abduction. But she was five seconds too late. As she rounded the corner of the tall red-brick building where Sickle had fallen, she had no way of knowing that the black limousine pulling away from the opposite kerb contained the unconscious body of her brother. It passed quite close to her as it swept around the corner, but its darkened windows kept the occupants hidden from view. Tia knew that, somehow or other, she had lost Tony. Now there was nothing else to do but retrace her steps and hope that Eddie would help her to search for him.

Fate, however, decreed otherwise. Eddie had returned to his cab shortly after Tia departed, and, believing the children had cheated him out of a fare, had gassed-up and driven angrily away. Tia arrived in time to see the rear of his cab disappear around the end of the street. She came to a halt on the sidewalk and stood still for a long time, looking helplessly around her. Now she'd not only lost Tony, but all her belongings as well.

Tia continued her search well into the afternoon. She wandered the streets aimlessly, hoping that she might pick up some telepathic contact with him. But it was not to be. Three hours and countless city blocks later, Tia found herself seated on an upturned crate outside a warehouse, a long way from the street where she had last seen her brother. She was tired, depressed and close to tears. What had caused her brother's strange disappearance? And how was she ever going to find him again? Where could she . . .

Her train of thought was rudely interrupted, as a series of shouts rang out from farther along the side of the warehouse.

'Get off the streets!'

'Run!'

'Hide!'

'Here come the Golden Goons!'

Tia looked up. Charging towards her came a group of four boys, looking as though a typhoon was whipping at their heels. They were roughly dressed, and were slightly older than Tia – but not as old (and certainly nowhere near as big) as the trio of tough-looking youths who were hounding them. As they approached, they waved their arms wildly at Tia and yelled again for her to take cover. Confused, surprised and without really knowing why (perhaps it was a natural reaction), Tia leapt to her feet and raced along with them.

When the pursued group of youngsters reached the end of the street, they turned left. But they had hardly gone more than a few yards before stopping dead in their tracks. Ahead of them, two more mean-looking Golden Goons stood shoulder-to-shoulder, barring their way. There was a moment of awful indecision, then the four boys swivelled on their heels and sped off in the other direction, with Tia hard on their heels.

The chase continued on across the intersection and down a narrow sidestreet, with the longer strides of the Golden Goons slowly beginning to close the gap. But it was the appearance of yet another pair of Goons – from behind a wrecked, abandoned car at the end of the street – that finally trapped the running band of youngsters. Cut off in both directions, they had only one place left to flee: a narrow, unwelcoming alleyway that looked suspiciously like a dead end. There was nothing else for it. The five youngsters ducked into the narrow opening and kept their fingers crossed. Behind them, the walls of the alley echoed to the shouts of their pursuers.

Tia slid to a halt, as did her companions. The alley, as they had feared, was blind. A high brick wall rose before them, with equally tall fencing on either side. There was no way out. In desperation, the four boys dived behind a line of garbage cans that ran around the end of the alley, and Tia followed suit. They knew, of course, that they were only delaying the inevitable.

Seconds later, the fearsome Golden Goons arrived, determined to maintain their reputation as the meanest gang in the district. Swaggering, the seven of them moved in for the kill, spreading out to advance on the garbage cans in a long line. Behind the cans, Tia's companions, torn and bruised, clung to each other fearfully. 'We're gonna be finished!' said the boy nearest to Tia.

But he reckoned without the help of a young girl from Witch Mountain. Without warning, one of the garbage cans suddenly flipped on to its side and began to roll towards the line of Golden Goons. Before they had a chance to take evasive action, it was careering into them like a huge bowling ball, scattering them and dumping them head over heels like a line of wooden pins.

Tia's friends were as amazed as their enemies. They could hardly believe their eyes, and looked curiously around them, trying to decide who or what it was that had come to their defence. Finally, their gaze came to rest on Tia, who was looking at the fallen Goons with a knowing smirk on her face.

'She must've did it!' cried one of the boys. Tia turned her head to find her companions waving grate-fully to her. They didn't understand how this strange girl had managed to pull such an incredible stunt, but they were thankful none the less. Tia, for her part, knew that Uncle Bené wouldn't have approved, but she couldn't stand idly by in such a one-sided fight. Now, however, she would have to think of something else, for the Golden Goons were on their feet again, and angrier than ever.

'Let's give it to 'em!' growled their leader, smacking a huge fist into his open palm. And once more the Goons moved threateningly forward ...

Tia concentrated. An idea was forming in her mind. As the Goons advanced, she energized seven more garbage cans, and they began to tilt forward like the levelling barrels of a battery of cannon.

With a clang, their lids dropped to the ground. Next

second, a great salvo of evil-smelling garbage was launched towards the enemy. The Goons reeled as they took the full force of a horrible barrage of rotting vegetables and assorted rubbish. But as the hail subsided, they were on their feet and charging forward once again. It seemed that Tia would have to think of something even better if she wanted to stop them.

This time, she energized the empty garbage cans and raised them into the air upside down. For a moment, they hovered above the astonished Goons, and then they suddenly shot downwards, dropping on top of their heads in a succession of dull clangs. It did the trick. The dazed Goons staggered blindly around, banging into each other, crashing into the walls, and struggling in vain to lift the heavy cans off their bruised heads. Their howls of pain sounded hollow and metallic, as one by one they tripped and toppled to the ground.

Seizing their chance, the four boys leapt out from behind their protective screen of garbage cans and, taking Tia by the hand, weaved a path through the helpless Goons and raced off down the alley. They ran and ran and didn't stop until their legs refused to carry them any farther. Exhausted, they came to a halt beneath a bridge in the middle of a huge drainage area, well out of sight of their enemies. It was a minute or two before the sound of rasping breath subsided and the boys gathered around Tia to thank her for saving their skins.

'What's your name?' asked the shortest and youngest member of the group.

'Tia.'

'I'm Rocky,' came the reply, along with an outstretched hand and a wide, toothy grin.

'I'm Muscles,' said the next boy in line. The introduction was delivered in a slow, even voice. He was dark-haired, round-faced and had a slightly pudgy appearance. He wasn't really muscular at all, but from the way he held himself, it was clear to Tia that he thought his name was more than appropriate.

'Crusher,' said the next. He had a thick mop of fair hair whose fringe was held aloft by a pair of heavy black spectacles. He, too, obviously felt he was in line for the next 'Mr Universe' title.

'. . . and I'm Dazzler,' said the last – and tallest – boy of all. He had a chunky, rugged look about him, with bright eyes and a chin that stuck forward in a cheeky, aggressive manner.

All of them wore short denim jackets which had been roughly relieved of their sleeves, with crumpled sweat shirts underneath. Studded leather wristlets on each of their forearms completed the uniform. They looked a motley group, but Tia had an idea that they were not nearly so tough as they made themselves out to be.

Dazzler took a deep breath and assumed a serious expression. He looked Tia straight in the eyes. 'We're the Earthquake Gang,' he said proudly, with enormous stress on the word 'Earthquake'. He sounded as though he were announcing that World War III had just begun.

'Does that scare you?' said Muscles.

Tia smiled. 'No,' she said honestly.

Rocky grimaced. 'Let's change our name again,' he said disappointedly. 'Gotta have a name that scares.'

'Hey,' chipped in Crusher, changing the subject, 'how did you do what you done?'

Tia shrugged. 'Oh … I really didn't do anything,' she said.

'You a magician or something?' asked Dazzler.

'No.'

'Wanna join our gang?' Crusher could see great advantage in having Tia join the Earthquakes. Even the Golden Goons might think twice about arguing with them again. But Tia had to decline the offer. 'I'm sorry,' she replied, 'but I'm looking for someone. Thank you anyway.'

'Yeah,' said Muscles, dropping his eyes to the ground. 'I guess you're like the rest of them. You musta heard that we're a nothin' gang.'

'We aint always gonna be nothin',' Dazzler corrected. 'Someday we're gonna be the toughest . . . take over this whole territory.'

Crusher nodded. 'Some day they're gonna run when they see us comin' down the block.'

Tia held a hand up in apology. She hadn't meant to offend them. 'It's just that I'm trying to find my brother,' she explained.

'What gang does he belong to?' asked Rocky.

'He doesn't belong to any gang.'

'Never heard of a guy who didn't belong to a gang,' said Crusher incredulously.

'I'm sure something's happened to him,' said Tia worriedly. 'I've got to find him.'

It wasn't hard to detect the edge of desperation that had crept into Tia's voice. Muscles put a comforting arm around her shoulder. 'If anybody can find him, we can,' he said sympathetically. 'We know this town inside out.'

Tia could hardly believe her luck. 'Would you?' she asked.

'Sure,' confirmed Dazzler. 'You done us a big favour. Now we'll do one for you.'

'Oh, thank you,' beamed Tia gratefully. 'Thank you

very much.' She shook each of the Earthquakes' hands in turn. At last, things were beginning to look up. After such a dismal morning: losing Tony, missing the cab, and the long hours of fruitless searching that followed, Tia had come close to despair. Now, with the help of the Earthquakes, she had a real chance of finding her brother again. So the group of youngsters moved back on to the street, laughing and joking and set to take over the whole city. For, with Tia amongst them, who was to say that the Earthquakes couldn't do just that?

The big search began. But Tony – wherever he was – had been well hidden. Even the Earthquake Gang, who knew the city well enough to find their way about it with their eyes closed, were unable to find him. By mid-afternoon, they were growing tired and beginning to give up hope.

Tia had become depressed and returned to wondering whether she was ever going to see her brother again. The Earthquakes horsed around in an effort to cheer her up, but it didn't seem to do much good. Moreover, when Muscles suggested that they walked Tia home, he only made matters worse, for it was then Tia remembered that she didn't have the address of the hotel which Uncle Bené had booked for her. It had been lost along with the note given to Eddie the cab-driver. Now, to top it all, she had nowhere to spend the night.

Then Dazzler had a brainwave. The Earthquakes – in keeping with all the best gangs – had a secret hideout. Why couldn't Tia stay there for the time being? It might not be as comfortable as a hotel, but it would be much more fun. And, if the gang didn't find Tony today, perhaps they could all try again tomorrow. They could go about their search in a more organized fashion, starting where Tia and her brother had last seen each other.

It was the perfect solution and Tia agreed gratefully. If nothing else had gone right today, at least she was lucky to have found such helpful friends. The youngsters headed on down the street. They decided to continue their search for another hour or so and then, if they still had no luck, to call it a day.

They had no way of knowing, however, that their quest was about to come to a sudden end much sooner than that – and in a most surprising way.

The group had just stepped off the sidewalk at the intersection when it happened. If the Earthquakes had had their wits about them, then perhaps they might have noticed the dark-green minibus which had been kerb-crawling behind them for the last two or three blocks. As it was, they were totally off-guard when the vehicle suddenly accelerated and screeched to a halt in front of them. Yelping, they leapt back on to the sidewalk. Tia just had time to read the words 'Board of Education' painted in bold white letters across the side of the vehicle, before the driver's door swung open and a man jumped down to confront them. Arms outstretched he advanced menacingly on the startled youngsters.

'It's Yoyo!' gasped Crusher.

Mr Yokomoto – or 'Yoyo' as he was affectionately known by the Earthquakes – was a short, stocky man with round shoulders and a battered leather jacket that looked like it was a size too big for him. He was in his middle years and his pudgy face was heavily lined and frozen in a permanently sad expression. Lunging forward, he made a wild grab for his prey. 'Okay kids,' he yelled. 'It's all over!'

But it wasn't, by any means. Yoyo was far too slow.

Dazzler found time to tug Tia out of reach and then the gang turned on their heels and hared off down the street. Yoyo was left clutching at thin air. 'Come back!' he shouted, starting after them. But he had already missed his chance.

Just the same, the Earthquakes kept going until they were well out of sight. A couple of blocks later, as they ducked through a gap in some fencing, Tia found time to ask: 'Who was that?'

'Our worst enemy!' said Dazzler breathlessly.

'The truant officer,' explained Muscles.

'He's tryin' to make us go back to school,' Rocky said, with a look of horror on his face. Tia had the impression that, given the choice, Rocky would rather face the Golden Goons alone and unaided in a dark alley, than face the fate Mr Yokomoto had in store for him.

They paused for a while, to catch their breath. It had been a narrow squeak, no doubt about that, and now they were all quite exhausted. Tia smiled wryly to herself. Being chased around this city was developing into a full-time hazard...

The Earthquakes' hideout proved to be something very special. It was dusk by the time Tia set eyes on it – the time at which the building probably looked its most impressive. The rambling, nineteenth-century dwelling rose up like a phantom from the desolate wasteground which surrounded it. It was the sole surviving structure on the block – everything else had been razed to the ground by the wrecker's ball. In the fading half-light, it would have been easy to believe that some demon's curse lay over the house, preserving it from all harm.

Tia and the gang picked their way carefully through

the rubble towards the house. As they reached the porch, Tia noticed with amusement that the boys had bunched quite closely together. She even fancied she saw Muscles shiver a little, although the evening air was still quite warm.

Dazzler pushed on the large front door and it creaked open. The youngsters stepped through. Inside it was dark and musty, with one or two square patches of grey light filtering in through the windows. Their eyes took a moment or two to adjust to the gloom. Motioning, Dazzler led the way across the floorboards and up a wide, uncarpeted staircase. It groaned under the gang's collective weight. Tia half expected to see a certain tall figure with heavy boots and a bolt through his neck coming to greet them. 'What time do the ghosts get here?' she asked, as much in an effort to break the eerie silence as anything. 'Don't say things like that,' said Crusher, looking nervously behind him.

They climbed on up to the second floor without another word. Dazzler pushed open another door and Tia found herself standing in a large, dark room. Muscles struck a match and a kerosene lamp popped into life, spilling a dim circle of light over the long wooden table on which it was standing. The room was sparsely furnished: some ragged mattresses and a small bunk bed grouped in a corner, a few rickety chairs, a rectangle of threadbare carpet and a pair of old blankets serving as drapes for the solitary window. Cobwebs and peeling wallpaper provided the decoration. The light from the lamp threw flickering patterns on the wall and dark shadows under the youngsters' eyes.

Tia wasn't very impressed. 'Is this it?' she asked.
'This is where we're gonna live when we run away

from home,' explained Dazzler proudly. 'You can't be a tough guy and take orders from your mother or older sister.'

'That's why we quit school,' chipped in Muscles. 'You can't be tough and educated too.' Tia was about to suggest that spooky hideouts like this one wouldn't necessarily make you tough either, but when she opened her mouth to speak, something entirely different came out. 'Tony!' she cried at the top of her voice.

The Earthquakes jumped back in fright. Tia's hands had shot up to her forehead and she was staring wide-eyed straight ahead of her.

'Where?' said Rocky, looking uneasily around the room. 'Where?'

Tia closed her eyes and screwed up her face in concentration. After a moment, she began to slowly rotate, like a radar scanner searching for a signal. The Earthquakes watched her, frozen to the spot and utterly mystified.

'I had contact . . .' Tia began. 'Just for a second . . .'

Rocky swallowed. 'She's weird,' he whispered.

'She's creepy,' added Crusher.

Tia held up her hand to silence her friends. She was making contact again. Yes. There was a light – a very fierce, intense light. There were hazy shapes, too, but she couldn't make any sense of them. She must concentrate harder. Were the shapes human? It was difficult to tell, for the light was so strong. And now the signal was fading again – she had lost her chance. '*Tony . . . where are you?*' she called desperately.

Dazzler shuddered. 'I ain't so sure I wanna meet this Tony,' he said.

The Earthquakes huddled together protectively. They continued to look on in amazement as, for the third time, Tia began to make contact with her brother. It was as if she were trying to tune in on a radio station whose signal persisted in dying away every few seconds. But now she was getting it again. Clearer than before – but still that blinding light was obscuring everything from view. Tia's face was contorted in a mixture of anguish and concentration. Why couldn't her brother make a positive telepathic contact? Why did the signal keep fading away? And why couldn't she see beyond this blazing, dazzling light?

3 The Experiment

Letha Wedge watched the pulsating light with rapt fascination.

She was standing in Victor Gannon's laboratory, located in a cavernous underground vault directly beneath the Wedge mansion, which stood on a hillside on the eastern outskirts of the city. The laboratory was furnished with some of the most expensive equipment money could buy – all of which had been supplied by Letha. Strange, complex apparatus dotted the greystone walls and floor. Highly advanced instrumentation lined rows of polished metal benches. In the centre stood an operating table, complete with all its sensitive machinery.

It was on this table that Tony was lying, eyes closed and held tightly in place by two wide leather straps. He was naked from the waist up. Small circular pads were attached to his forehead and chest and from these a profusion of wires snaked away to lose themselves in a variety of humming electronic devices. Needles flickered on gauges and coloured lights flashed on panels. Overhead, the cluster of frosted spotlights that provided the operating table with its main source of illumination was continually brightening and dimming, like a flashing neon sign.

'Is *he* doing that?' asked Letha disbelievingly. Gannon nodded, equally amazed. 'He's projecting a magnetic field through his reflexes, as he struggles for consciousness,' he explained. 'His output is so great that my instruments aren't capable of measuring it.'

As if in agreement, one of the devices to which Tony was hooked began to vibrate ominously. The indicator needle wavered warningly in the red zone and the instrument's hum rose to a protesting wail. Gannon rushed to throw the master switch. He was too late. With a resounding bang and cascade of bright red flashes, the machine short-circuited.

Letha ducked, shielding her head with her hands. 'He's dangerous!' she yelled.

Gannon picked himself up from the floor. 'Once I have control of his brain,' he scoffed, 'he'll only be dangerous to others.' Like a man possessed, he strode quickly across the laboratory towards the prostrate form of Sickle, who was lying in a semi-dazed condition on another table.

He reached behind Sickle's ear and set about the delicate task of removing the tiny electronic receptor he had placed there earlier. 'With these receptors and the boy's powers combined,' he gloated, 'I'll become one of the most influential men in the world.'

Letha smiled. 'Then perhaps we can move forward with some of my plans, too,' she prompted.

Gannon scowled. 'Don't bother me with your plans,' he said irritably. 'They're empty and unimportant.'

Letha's mouth set in a taut line. She was deeply offended. True, Victor was a scientific genius and the real brains of the outfit, but that didn't mean he could insult her when he felt like it. After all, it was Letha's money which had gone to setting up this laboratory. In doing so, she had got herself in debt up to her neck. Gannon, of course, had contributed nothing. Indeed, he had no money of his own, for he had been out of employment for years. Outlawed by his fellow scientists for his dangerous experiments, he had journeyed the length of the country, trying to find someone to sponsor him in his search for the secret of mind-control. No one would accommodate him – no one that is, until he met the ambitious Letha, who saw in his ideas the way to a fortune beyond her wildest dreams. It was said that Letha Wedge would gamble her entire wealth on two raindrops running down a window-pane – and there was more than a little truth in this. Consequently, she needed little persuasion to accept the exhilarating gamble that Gannon's mind-control presented. The bargain had been struck: Letha would supply the money, and Gannon would perfect his amazing device. Then he would use it to make Letha fabulously rich.

The problem was, now that he had succeeded, Gannon appeared more interested in power than riches. It was a trait which irritated Letha, for she hungered only for money. Enough of it to make her the richest woman in the world.

She had just decided to put her arrogant partner straight on the matter, when a high-pitched noise caused them both to turn in the direction of the operating table. Another of the measuring devices had reached over-load. It whined hysterically for a second and then, with a loud crash, blew apart, sending fragments flying across the laboratory.

Gannon stopped what he was doing and hurried across to check on his instruments. The two that remained in operation, monitoring Tony's energy-field, were going wild. And now he could see why. Tony was regaining consciousness. His eyelids were flickering and he was trying to raise his head. Not yet, thought Gannon, not yet. He must not allow the boy to awaken before he had transplanted the receptor. There was no telling what might happen if he did.

Frantically, Gannon scrabbled away on a nearby bench for his hypodermic needle. Tony was coming round very quickly. But it wasn't quickly enough. Next moment Gannon had the needle in his grasp and was plunging it into his helpless victim's arm. For the second time that day, Tony sank back into the deep, bottomless well of oblivion.

The blinding light which Tia had seen so clearly, suddenly went out.

Listlessly, she moved to the bunk bed in the corner and sat down. She sighed heavily. Something told her that her brother wouldn't be resuming contact for some time. There was nothing she could do about it: she just had to wait. The most frustrating thing of all was that she hadn't been able to form any idea of his whereabouts. If only she had even a small clue ...

The Earthquakes gathered round to console her. But she was too tired and too upset to be consoled – even by good friends such as these. In the end, the boys decided it would be best to leave her alone. So they left quietly, promising to return in the morning with whatever food they could find, and the maps they needed to help them in their renewed search of the city. After they had gone, Tia sat for a long while staring blankly into the darkness. Eventually, she doused the kerosene lamp, lay down on the lumpy bed, and softly cried herself to sleep.

Thankfully, she slept soundly and without dreams. She awoke eight hours later to the sounds of the Earthquakes entering the house and stomping up the staircase. She got up and tugged back the drapes. It was a fine day outside and the morning sun reached into the room to warm her and lift her spirits. She yawned and stretched widely. A second later, the door opened and her friends tumbled in, spilling a handful of smuggled food on to the table. Tia sat down to a hearty breakfast consisting of a slice of ham, three hardboiled eggs, four slices of cold toast and a carton of milk. It had been a long time since she had last eaten and the food tasted delicious.

While she ate, Muscles produced a detailed map of the city from his jacket pocket and spread it on the table. He quickly pinpointed the location where Tia had last seen her brother and the group got down to an argument on how best to conduct the day's search. The city looked a dauntingly large place – and they had so little to go on. For his part, Crusher said he didn't mind how they planned the operation, so long as there was a good chance of a rumble with someone on the way. He punched the air playfully to show he meant business. He reckoned this must have looked pretty tough, although he secretly hoped that Tia wouldn't suggest going anywhere near the Golden Goon territory again...

He needn't have worried. Tia wasn't about to suggest anything. She was sitting bolt upright in her chair, with a partially eaten slice of toast held halfway to her mouth. Her eyes were tightly closed.

'Here we go again ...' said Rocky, watching Tia apprehensively. He was getting familiar with the symptoms of Tia's trances. The Earthquakes stood absolutely still, waiting to see what would happen.

Tia was making contact again, and this time the images were much sharper than before. She furrowed her brow in concentration. She fancied she heard a man's voice. A deep voice, which had a ring of authority about it. And yes – she could see strange machines and instruments, of the kind you might expect to find in...

'... a hospital,' she said slowly. 'Tony's in a room somewhere ... and it looks like a hospital ...'

'This is Doctor Gannon,' said the voice. 'I command you to awaken.'

Tony's eyes snapped open. He was still strapped tightly to the operating table in Gannon's laboratory, but the tangle of wires and electronic sensors was gone. The only device attached to him now was Gannon's tiny receptor, which had been carefully installed behind his right ear.

His mind was a complete blank; he had no memory and he could not seem to marshal his thoughts. He was aware only of a powerful outside influence that was sapping his will – and of a voice which he had to obey.

Now it was speaking again. 'You will function exclusively under my control,' intoned Gannon. He was standing close to the table, holding the control unit to his mouth. At his shoulder Letha stood poised with the hypodermic needle, ready to pounce if the patient showed any signs of non-cooperation. 'All thinking and reasoning will be done by the voice that commands you,' continued the doctor. 'Do you understand?'

'Yes,' answered Tony flatly.

'What is your name?'

'Tony.'

'Where are you from?'

'Witch Mountain.'

'Must be a hick town,' chipped in Sickle who was cautiously observing proceedings from the far side of the table.

'How did you suspend Mr Sickle in mid-air?' pressed Gannon.

'By energizing matter.' Tony's voice was characterless, mechanical.

'Do you mean to say you can control molecular flow?'

'Yes.'

'How did you learn to do this?'

'I was born with the ability.'

Gannon thought for a moment. 'I wish to see a demonstration,' he said finally. 'You are strapped to the table. I command you to unbuckle yourself!'

Obediently, Tony raised his head. The straps pinning him to the table were held together by large metal buckles. As the assembled company looked on in amazement, Tony energized the buckles and the straps slipped gently apart, dropping down to hang at the side of the table. Tony sat up.

'Excellent! Excellent!' beamed Gannon. 'You have fantastic potential.' He turned to Letha, triumphantly. 'A power has come into my hands centuries ahead of its time. We must use it wisely.' Letha looked a little bemused. 'What will we have him do?' she asked. 'Go around making people's belts open?' Gannon snorted in disgust at Letha's inability to appreciate this scientific wonder. 'The possibilities are unlimited,' he assured her.

Sickle shrugged sceptically. 'It's just some kind of gimmick, that's all,' he sneered.

Gannon raised his eyebrows in mock query. He couldn't abide fools. It was high time this one was taught a lesson. He glanced around the laboratory, looking for inspiration. Suddenly, an idea came to him. 'Tony,' he said pensively into the control unit, 'Mr Sickle – whose life you saved – still doesn't believe in you. He's tired, physically and mentally. He should rest. Help him sleep Tony. Give him a snoot full of ether.' Gannon nodded towards an anaesthetic stand positioned at the head of the operating table and Tony followed his gaze. Next moment, the four tiny rubber wheels on which it was mounted began moving the stand in Sickle's direction. The rubber mask on top of the ether cylinder detached itself and, trailing its flexible hose behind it, reached out towards Sickle's face. 'Hey, wait a minute ...' cried Sickle, anxiously backing away. 'Wait a minute ...'

The mobile cylinder bore down on him, the black rubber mask floating in mid-air, ready to pounce like a striking cobra. Sickle managed to dodge the first attack, ducking behind one of the benches. He yelled for Gannon to turn it off but the doctor simply smiled as the cylinder swung slowly round and began the pursuit all over again.

Letha watched with an expression of amusement and sheer wonderment on her face. She was still doubtful, however. 'I can see how he'd be a big hit at a scientific convention,' she posed, 'but the bottom line is: how do we make money out of him?'

Gannon shook his head. The trouble with Letha, he thought, was that she didn't know how to apply her imagination. 'Let me demonstrate an industrial application,' suggested Gannon. With that he steered both Tony and Letha out of the laboratory, down a flight of steps and into the wine cellar. Behind them, they left the loudly protesting Sickle frenziedly dodging between the benches in his efforts to evade the relentless ether cylinder.

The wine cellar was large and well stocked. Letha had an appetite for good food and fine wines surpassed only by her appetite for the money which supplied them. Row upon row of bottles and wooden casks were neatly arranged around the walls of the cellar.

Off to one side, a number of casks stood upright on the cold stone floor. They were newly delivered and were awaiting proper storage. 'Tony,' instructed Gannon, 'I want you to stack those wine casks neatly.'

It was a tricky operation, but Tony accomplished it faultlessly. One by one he energized the heavy casks and, manoeuvring them with great care, formed them into a neatly stacked pyramid. Letha watched the operation closely, clearly impressed with Tony's skill. 'And now,' continued Gannon, when the last cask had been levitated into position, 'you will serve us with two glasses of Burgundy.'

Accordingly, a pair of wine glasses detached themselves from a nearby shelf and glided smoothly through the air to suspend themselves beneath the spigots of two wine casks. The dark red liquid flowed into the glasses. Another gentle flight across the cellar brought them safely into the outstretched hands of Gannon and Letha. Not a drop of Burgundy had been spilt.

The two unlikely partners clinked glasses in a toast. 'To Molecular Mobilization!' smiled Gannon.

'To Molecular Mobilization!' echoed Letha. They tossed the wine down in one gulp and burst into a peal of laughter. They were on their way to power and riches untold.

A few yards away, back in the laboratory, Sickle found himself unable to join in the celebrations. He was sitting propped against the laboratory goat's cage, sleeping soundly, with the rubber mask from the anaesthetic stand clamped firmly over his face . . .

4 The Plan

Tia and the Earthquakes spent the day inquiring at every hospital in the city, to see if Tony had been admitted. Naturally, they drew a blank. Late afternoon found them back wandering the streets again, tired and uncertain how to continue their quest. Every so often Tia would pause in her stride and put a hand to her forehead in an effort to 'tune-in' on Tony's wavelength.

'She's been doin' that all day,' said Rocky, as Tia went through her telepathic ritual yet again.

'Maybe she's got a headache,' suggested Crusher dryly.

Dazzler came to Tia's side. 'Gettin' any clues?' he asked.

'Nothing at all,' replied Tia, opening her eyes. 'It's so strange. It's as if his mind is a complete blank.'

'He must be conked out,' concluded Crusher, somewhat tactlessly. This remark seemed to upset Tia, who looked as if she were about to break down. The strain of the last couple of days was beginning to tell on her, and the Earthquakes had been slow to appreciate it. Muscles gave Crusher a hard shove for his thoughtless comment and Dazzler put a comforting arm around Tia's shoulder. 'Don't listen to him,' he said reassuringly. 'We're gonna find Tony, for sure.' Muscles came over to take Tia's hand. 'Yeah,' he added sympathetically, 'we'll find him if we have to turn this town upside down.'

Tia managed to produce a wan smile. She knew the

Earthquakes meant well, but she also knew that, as time slipped by, the chances of finding her brother were growing slimmer and slimmer.

Letha's spacious study was in semi-darkness. The heavy, luxuriant drapes were drawn, shutting out the lights of the city and the cool white moon that hung in the sky above them. The highly polished oak-panelling shone dully with the yellow light of a solitary angle-poised lamp. Letha sat behind her desk, poring intently over a collection of papers and photographs.

Abruptly, the door of the study clicked open and a white rectangle imprinted itself on the thick pile carpet. Letha scrabbled to conceal her papers, then relaxed again as she saw the identity of her visitor. Sickle closed the door behind him. His lengthy, casual stride took him across to the desk in three easy steps. He perched himself on the edge of it. Nodding at the pile of documents, he said, 'Got the horses picked for tomorrow?'

Letha supported her chin in the heel of her right hand. 'I'm thinking,' she explained.

'Good. We need a couple of winners.'

'We already have a winner,' corrected Letha.

'The daily double?'

Letha shook her head condescendingly. 'My dear nephew,' she began, 'I'm talking about our new companion. Can you imagine for instance, what a day at the races with Tony would be like? Or an evening at the roulette table?' Sickle's slow-witted brain took two or three seconds to make the connection. 'You mean,' he answered slowly, 'that Tony could help us to win every ti—'

'Exactly,' interjected Letha. 'As Victor said, the possibilities are unlimited. Today he stacked the wine casks just by looking at them. Well, if he can stack things, he can unstack them too...' Letha selected a photograph from among the handful on her desk and passed it to her nephew. Her cold blue eyes watched him expectantly.

'What's this – gold?' Sickle frowned. The photograph depicted a large pyramid of gleaming yellow bars, encased in some kind of glass – or was it plastic? – bubble. 'Three million dollars' worth to be precise,' confirmed Letha. 'It's on display at the museum, just waiting for us to walk in and take it.' A wide smile spread across Sickle's angular face. 'You mean Gannon said it's okay to use the control and Tony?'

'No,' admitted Letha. 'But I own half the invention, and half of Tony. That means I own half the profits. So far, the return on my investment has been half of zero. It's high time we put that right.'

Sickle nodded reflectively. Then he studied the photograph again. 'What about the security,' he mused. 'We'd need an army to penetrate the kind of security they'd have for this.'

Letha spread her hands and smiling broadly, rose from her desk. 'But we'll have an army,' she pointed out. 'We'll have Tony.'

The following morning Letha's plan was put into action. Gannon had taken the Citroën into town to pick up some new equipment for his laboratory and had left a note saying that he would not be back for some time. Letha saw her chance. Dragging Sickle along with her, she slipped down to the laboratory and through to one of the small basement rooms where Tony was being kept prisoner.

Unlocking the door, they entered to find the boy sleeping soundly on the hard-looking bunk bed in the

45

corner. Next to him, on a low table, lay Gannon's miniature miracle: the mind-control unit. The blue light burning brightly on its panel of buttons showed that it was in neutral mode. Cautiously, Letha walked over and picked it up. She held it as though it were a grenade that might explode with the slightest mishandling.

'You sure you know how to use it?' said a worried Sickle.

'I'm very good with mechanical things,' Letha assured him, completely unaware that the device she held in her hands was about as mechanical as a quartz wristwatch. Gingerly, she selected a button marked 'transmit' and depressed it. Abruptly, the blue light went out, a green one came on and the unit began to make a low buzzing sound. It seemed to encourage her. Clearing her throat, she lifted the control unit to her mouth. 'Tony,' she said assertively, 'this is Letha Wedge. I command you to open your eyes.'

On cue, Tony's eyes popped open. Letha was almost as surprised as Sickle. Perhaps this thing wasn't as difficult to handle as she had thought. 'Stand up,' she ordered.

Obediently, Tony swung his legs from the bed and stood up. The same vacant stare still glazed his eyes. Letha smiled. The sense of power she felt was electrifying; she had no idea how exciting it could be. Relieving the city museum of three million dollars' worth of gold bars was going to be no problem at all . . .

With Letha at their head, the motley trio went up through the house and out to the garage. Sickle reversed out in the household's second car, a big yellow Ford. Letha and Tony got in and the car glided off down the hill towards the city.

Fifteen minutes later, Sickle braked gently to a halt

outside the museum. Letha clutched the control unit tightly in her elegant, black-gloved hands, the glint of gold already in her eyes. Quickly, she issued Sickle with his instructions: he was to remain with the car and be ready, with the trunk open and waiting for the delivery of the gold bars. She and Tony would do the rest. Sickle nodded. Letha and her submissive charge got out of the car and walked across the street towards the museum. They mounted the wide stone steps and went inside.

The exhibition – the theme of which was the great Gold Rush – was housed within the big square museum hall. Letha and Tony weaved their way into the maze of visitors and showpieces. The profusion of displays dealing with the mining, processing and coining of gold cleverly captured the atmosphere of the Old West – and all in lifesize. One display depicted the entry to a mine shaft, with dummy miners guiding ore carts along the track from the tunnel mouth. Another showed a man panning for gold in a stream. Yet another depicted an assay office, with all its attendant paraphenalia. There was even a detailed reconstruction of an assay furnace. Around the hall, lifelike figures of cowboys, pioneer women and American Indians were spaced between the major exhibits. A beautiful (but sadly horseless) stagecoach added the final touch of atmosphere to a well-planned exhibition.

The star of the show, of course, was the gold. It stood in the exact centre of the hall, a tall, shining pyramid of yellow bars, protected by a huge perspex bubble. One glance at it explained more about gold fever than all the other displays put together. Letha's pulse quickened at the thought that it would soon be hers. She scanned the hall to check out the security arrangements. A posse of uniformed guards (male and female) were sprinkled at strategic points around the hall, and two or three more moved constantly among the visitors. Four others were stationed around the perspex bubble. But this wasn't all. There were obviously complex electronic devices as well, for high up on the walls, Letha could see the narrow window of a security control box, and behind it a bank of machinery that reminded her of mission control, Houston.

She smiled wickedly. The security system hadn't been built that could stand against the force of Tony's molecule thingummy – or whatever it was Gannon said he possessed. She guided Tony into an alcove which was out of sight from the security box, a plan already forming in her mind. As inconspicuously as possible she lifted the control unit to her mouth. 'Tony,' she whispered, 'we're about to create a diversion. See that stagecoach' – his eyes swivelled towards it – 'I command you to make it roll around the hall!'

The long, heavy shaft which ran out between the front wheels of the stagecoach, began to raise itself a foot off the floor. The big spoked wheels began to turn. A man who had been standing close to the passenger door, peering inside, let out a yell of surprise and jumped back. Creaking and rattling, the stage began to pick up speed, carving a path into the astonished crowd. The security guards stared goggle-eyed as it began to circle the perspex bubble.

Letha was so excited that she almost dropped the control unit. Already, the guards were stunned. Now she must add to the confusion whilst she had the chance. Quickly she spun Tony around to face another exhibit: the one depicting the entrance to a mine. 'Make the ore carts chase the security guards,' she commanded.

Tony obeyed. Three metal wagons, each served by a dummy miner, detached themselves from the railway track and rolled off towards their targets. A stern-faced female guard squealed in anguish as one of the carts latched on to her. Frantically, she tried to outrun it, but it was much too fast for her. She turned and leapt sideways, but misjudged her footing and went sailing backwards into another display. The dummy kneeling by a stream suddenly found its sifting pan full of 130 pounds of struggling security guard.

Letha stifled an evil laugh. The museum was in uproar. But there was yet more fun to be had. 'Activate the dummies,' she ordered.

Tony did so. The dummy of the man panning for gold suddenly rose to its feet, jerking its pan and the woman guard inside it high into the air. She flung her arms about its neck for support. A few yards away, a dummy Indian sprang to life and strode boldly into the crowd, tomahawk raised. More and more of the manikins were energized. One of the guards found himself threatened by a cowboy with a shotgun and took to his heels, only to find himself headed off by one of the flying ore carts. It scooped him up and shot off into the mouth of the mine shaft.

The crowd didn't know what to expect next. Was this a publicity stunt, a mass hallucination, or had the world gone mad? Many of them decided not to wait and find out. Consequently, the two exit doors became rapidly clogged with milling, shouting people. High up in his control box, the security controller looked down into the body of the hall, absolutely aghast. Below him, the stagecoach thundered on and on around the gold display, the ore carts zigzagged across the floor, and the dummies chased after his startled guards. He closed his eyes and shook his head to try and make the nightmare go away.

'Gold!' yelled Tia.

By now, the Earthquakes were growing accustomed to these sudden aberrations. When this particular one occurred, they were out searching the streets as usual, no more than half a mile from the city museum. They paused to see if Tia could maintain the contact this time.

'I can see gold . . .' repeated Tia, concentrating, 'and wait . . . yes . . . there's also a stagecoach.'

'Must be tuned into a western,' Muscles surmised, nudging Rocky playfully.

Dazzler gestured for the gang to be quiet. It had been more than a day since Tia had last made contact with her brother, and he didn't want her to lose it now.

'I can see . . . dummies,' continued Tia. Muscles was about to point out that he didn't need to close his eyes to see the three dummies standing next to him, but thought better of it. Tia was clearly on to something now.

'There's old clothing . . . old furniture,' she muttered. Dazzler snapped his fingers. 'The Salvation Army!' he concluded. Crusher shook his head. 'They don't got stagecoaches at the Salvation Army,' he reminded. 'And they don't got gold neither,' added Rocky.

Dazzler shrugged in reluctant agreement. Where in the world might two such unlikely items be found together? He racked his brain for a solution. He hadn't thought so hard since he was at school. Hang on – that was it, he had the answer! 'I've got it!' he cried, jumping into the air. 'That lousy school we go to . . . we had one of them nothin' class trips to the museum...' Muscles' eyes lit up. 'I remember that trip,' he interrupted. 'I played hooky from it.'

'They got a big pile of gold,' continued Dazzler, 'and a stagecoach! They hadda chase me outta it!'

Tia bubbled over with excitement. At last she had pinpointed Tony's location! Her eyes, which had been so dull and vacant for the last two days, now held the glint of renewed hope. She grabbed Dazzler by the arm. 'Let's get going!' she demanded.

As one, the Earthquakes turned and ran off down the street. Only Rocky grimaced at the thought of their half-mile dash to the museum. 'Aw,' he moaned, 'this all sounds too edjacational to me.'

5 The Heist

Chaos reigned at the museum. The diversion was working even better than Letha had dared hope – but there was still more to do before entering upon the next phase of her plan.

'Tony,' she commanded, 'make the security system break down!'

Tony's head lifted. Up in the security box, the controller had snapped out of his momentary inaction and was reaching for a switch on his bank of instruments. Once thrown, it would activate a hydraulic mechanism which would lower the gold bars into the basement, safe from any attempted robbery. Tony's energizing power, however, was as fast as the speed of thought. The controller could do nothing but stare in horror as his equipment began to disintegrate around him. A blizzard of electrical components, metal fragments and tangled wires blew swiftly through the security box, accompanied by a deluge of sparks. Five seconds later all that remained of his sophisticated instrumentation was a pile of unrecognizable, smouldering junk. The controller picked himself up off the floor, still clutching the switch he had been holding before the explosion.

Down on the floor of the hall the bright flash of red light behind the security-box window had given Letha yet another idea. 'Ignite the furnace,' she demanded.

Tony swung to face his next target. Abruptly, the reconstruction furnace flared into life. Two guards rushed to extinguish it, but found themselves intercepted by the scuttling ore carts. There was no time to dodge out of the way. The guards were toppled sideways into the carts and carried off around the hall, legs thrashing the air.

Meanwhile, one of their colleagues had decided to try his luck at stopping the stagecoach. It was rolling fast enough now for the wheel-spokes to have disappeared in a blur, but that didn't deter him. Showing tremendous fitness for his middle years, the guard bounded across the hall on an interception course that brought him just a yard or so in front of the runaway stage. His timing was good. As the stage drew level, he reached out and grabbed for a hold. His fingers locked around the edge of the driving-seat and he hauled himself up into position. So far, so good, he thought. John Wayne couldn't have done better himself. But now what? He snatched up the reins and heaved on them, but it seemed to have no effect. How could it, when there were no horses to respond to his tugging? Suddenly, the guard heard a loud thud behind him and twisted around. What he saw was enough to make him forget all about his problems with the reins. Hanging on to the back of the stagecoach, tomahawk thrust forward, was the dummy Indian. Its war-painted face sent a chill down his spine. As he watched, horrified, it began to inch slowly towards him across the roof. He searched hurriedly for some kind of weapon with which to defend himself, but found nothing. In desperation, he grabbed for his peaked cap, with the intention of throwing it. But it had long since parted company with him and what came off in his right hand was a small mop of dark brown hair: his toupee. There was nothing else for it; the Indian was getting closer. Panic-stricken, the guard tossed his toupee at the dummy and jumped for it. He hit the floor, scrambled to his feet and raced off towards the exit. He'd had enough. They'd told him he'd been hired to look after a pile of gold, not to fight hostile Indians!

Back on top of the stagecoach, the dummy Indian's tomahawk had claimed its first scalp.

The dummy cowboys were creating their share of havoc, too. In one corner of the hall, two of them with shotguns had rounded up a whole group of security guards, who held their hands high in abject surrender.

The pandemonium was at its peak. People rushed everywhere. The stage thundered round and round. The ore carts whizzed to and fro. The guards struggled with the dummies. The assay furnace flared. And to cap it all, the electronic security system had been completely blown out of commission. It was total confusion.

Now, Letha decided, it was time for phase two. Methodically, she directed her young partner's gaze towards the central exhibit. 'Tony,' she purred, 'I want you to make a hole in the perspex shield.'

As if hit by some invisible heat ray, the top of the transparent plastic dome suddenly began to bubble and melt away to form a ragged hole about five feet in diameter. Letha could feel the gold bars already. 'Now,' she directed, 'levitate the bars, fly them out of the front door, and deliver them to Mr Sickle at the car!'

Slowly, smoothly, the bar on top of the pyramid rose upwards through the hole in the perspex shield. It soared gracefully across the hall towards the exit. At intervals of about five yards, the others began to follow on. The security guards (those who were still on their feet) couldn't believe their eyes. Self-propelled stagecoaches were one thing – but flying gold bars?

Outside on the sidewalk, Sickle rubbed his hands

together in anticipation as the first of the bars came into sight. He was standing by the open trunk of the Ford, ready and waiting to load up, as instructed. 'Come on, millions!' he whispered delightedly as the first bar sailed smoothly down towards him. He reached out and caught it easily in his right hand. He misjudged the weight, however, and it threw him just a little off-balance. From that moment onwards, things started to go wrong.

By the time he recovered and turned to place the bar in the trunk, the second one was almost upon him. Quickly, he transferred the first bar to his left hand and caught the second with his right. But he almost dropped it. Before he could load either of the bars, number three came gliding down and thudded into his ribcage. He yelped with pain and tried to cradle the gold bars in his arms, but things were getting out of control. Then the fourth bar drove solidly into his stomach, knocking the wind out of him. Thrown completely off-balance, he fell back against the car, accidently slamming the trunk lid closed. Now he was really in trouble. More and more bars were filing through the air towards him, and as yet he hadn't loaded a single one. He twisted round and began struggling madly to re-open the trunk. Another bar punched into his right shoulder. Wincing with pain, he turned just in time to avoid the next, which landed with a hefty crunch on the lid of the trunk. The following bar came in at head-height. He ducked just in time, but was unable to stop the bar crashing right through the rear window. It sailed on through the car and, smashing out the windshield, finally came to a metal-denting halt on the hood. By this time the slow machine-gun volley of gold was unstoppable. Sickle fought frantically to protect himself from the battering bars, but it was a battle he couldn't hope to win.

Inside the museum, Letha was about to make her nephew's predicament worse. The pyramid of gold bars had been reduced by about a third now, but it wasn't moving fast enough for her liking. 'Tony,' she commanded, 'get the rest of it out there faster!'

Obediently, Tony energized the remainder of the gold. The lower bulk of the pyramid lifted clear of the plastic shield and began its journey out of the hall, into the street and towards the beleaguered Sickle.

It was at this moment that Tia and the Earthquakes arrived outside the museum. They paused for a second to crane their necks in amazement as the wealth of precious metal passed overhead. Tia was the first to react. 'Tony's here!' she exclaimed. 'I know it!' Without further ado, she bounded on up the museum steps and began threading her way through the crowd to the main hall. The Earthquakes raced after her.

Inside the hall, the youngsters came to a halt. It was quite clear to Tia who was responsible for such confusion.

'Hey – look out lady!' shouted Rocky. A woman dressed in a large, heavy skirt and an old-fashioned hat almost pushed him over as she pressed towards the door. 'Why don'cha watch where you're ...' Rocky's voice trailed off as he caught sight of the woman's face. It was fixed in a cold unmoving stare. In fact, her whole body was as rigid as her face. She was a dummy.

Rocky's eyes popped wide and he leapt backwards, throwing his arms around Crusher's neck. Crusher tried to fight him off. Muscles and Dazzler just stood frozen to the spot, totally amazed at what was going on.

Tia, however, reacted with lightning speed. Reversing the molecular flow, she threw the master switch on Tony's mischievous activities. Everything that had been under her brother's control was abruptly de-energized. The stagecoach and the ore carts coasted to a stop. The roving dummies froze. The assay furnace died.

The sudden inaction took everybody by surprise. Guards and visitors came to a stunned standstill. For a long moment they were all quite uncertain how to react.

'What happened?' asked Letha disbelievingly.

'Molecular flow reversed,' came Tony's computer-like response.

'Did you do it?'

'No.'

'Then who did?'

'It would have to be one of my people.'

Letha frowned. 'You mean there are more like you?' she queried. An edge of concern had crept into her voice.

'Yes.'

Oh no, thought Letha. Not another Tony. She couldn't afford complications at this stage – not after having engineered such a perfect robbery. Not when she had three million beautiful dollars almost within her grasp. 'Let's get out of here!' she called, pulling Tony towards the exit.

That was when Tia caught sight of her brother for the first time since she had lost him three days ago. 'Tony!' she yelled.

'Who's that?' said Letha, turning in the direction of Tia's shout. On the far side of the hall, she could make out the diminutive figure of a blonde-haired girl, looking imploringly across towards them. Tony didn't answer immediately. As Letha watched, a faint glimmer of recognition flickered across his face. He put a hand to his forehead, as if in pain. Somewhere deep down in his subconscious, his will struggled to break free. 'My sister . . .' he said haltingly. 'My sister, Tia.'

'This is no time for family reunions!' snapped Letha and turning quickly, hustled Tony out of the hall. Behind them, Tia was crestfallen. She couldn't understand why her brother hadn't responded to her. It wasn't like him at all. And who was that strange woman who was telling him what to do? 'Tony, it's me!' called Tia and started after her brother at a run, with the Earthquakes hard on her heels.

Outside, Letha and Tony came to a sudden halt at the top of the steps. Across the street, their getaway car looked more like a relic from a demolition derby than the stylish saloon it had once been. The big Ford squatted low on its suspension, wheels splayed outwards under the crushing weight of the pyramid of gold bars that now sat untidily on the trunk lid.

The windows were shattered and the doors, wings, roof and hood were peppered with huge dents. Underneath the car, just visible amongst the debris, lay Sickle, with hands clasped protectively over his head.

Letha gaped stupidly. Now what? Without transport, there could be no hope of getting away. Soon, the police would be here and then . . .

'You fool!' The voice rang out like a rifle shot above the background noises of confusion and clanging bells. There was no mistaking the deep, authoritative tone. Letha turned to meet the cold stare of Victor Gannon, who had one foot on the bottom of the steps. He looked as if he might explode at any moment. 'How could you do this?' he boomed angrily.

Letha didn't know whether to feel fear or relief. How had Gannon traced her here? She checked herself; the question was unimportant, at least for the time being. The pressing issue was getting away, and Letha could see their sleek Citroën parked just a few yards farther down the street. 'We'll argue later,' she said, coming down the steps. 'Let's get going. Tony's sister is right behind us.'

Gannon was taken aback, confused. He was furious with Letha for abducting Tony, but even he could see that this was not the time or place to vent his rage. He fell in with Letha's suggestion, and the three of them made hurried tracks towards the Citroën. At the same time, a bruised and battered Sickle emerged from beneath the Ford, and sped across the street to join them.

A second later, Tia and the Earthquakes stumbled out of the museum and came to a halt on the steps. 'Tony!' called Tia desperately, 'Tony! Tony!' But it was no use. Her brother was paying no attention to her urgent cries. Worse still, there was no chance of catching up with him now, as he was being bundled hastily into a shiny black limousine, some fifty yards down the street.

The doors of the Citroën slammed shut. Sickle was behind the wheel (his accustomed place) and Letha was beside him. Gannon and Tony settled into the back seat. As Sickle fumbled with the ignition keys, Letha's eyes fell on the handful of photographs that were lying on top of the dashboard. So that was it. Gannon must have returned early to the house, found Tony missing, and gone to see if Letha was in her study. Then he had found the photographs of the museum on her desk, and simply put two and two together. Well, thought Letha philosophically, perhaps it was just as well he had. Without the Citroën, the three of them would have been dead ducks by now for sure.

Sickle turned the key and the big, powerful engine purred into life. He slammed the gear lever into first, gunned the revs, and took his foot off the clutch. But nothing happened. There was no surge of power, no squeal of tyres. Just a quiet spluttering noise, a jolt, and then ... standstill. Sickle grimaced in irritation. He reached forward and twisted the key again. Nothing.

'What's the matter?' asked Gannon.

'I don't know! I keep this car runnin' perfect!' answered Sickle, perplexed.

It was true. What Sickle lacked in the way of grey matter, he made up for in mechanical know-how. He always kept the Citroën's engine tuned to perfection. He couldn't understand what had gone wrong.

Letha had figured it out, however. For the past few seconds, she had been looking in the rear-view mirror, and now she twisted around to jab a finger at Tony, whose face was as expressionless as ever. 'It's his sister,' she proclaimed. 'She did it. She's as weird as he is.'

Gannon looked out of the rear window. He could see that Letha was right. It was hard to believe, but the slim, freckle-faced young girl standing on the museum steps was actually preventing their vehicle from moving! Well, no matter. He held the remedy in his hands. Lifting the control unit to his mouth, he said, 'Tony ... I command you to make the motor of this car run perfectly and continuously, without interference from your sister.'

No sooner said than done. With alarming suddenness, the engine roared with power. Even Sickle's sensitive foot on the clutch couldn't prevent the car from taking off like a souped-up rocket. The Citroën catapulted down the street, throwing its passengers back into their seats with the force of its acceleration.

Tia and the Earthquakes stood watching helplessly as it sped into the distance. At this range, Tony's control over the car's engine far outweighed Tia's. She sighed in frustration. A minute ago, she had almost been close enough to touch him, but now she was back where she started.

6 The Chase

Luck, or a change of fortune, can sometimes arrive in the strangest guises. Like finding out that a dreaded visit to the dentist occurs on the same afternoon as that tough history test your class is having at school. Or sorting out some old jeans in which to clean up the backyard, and coming across a dollar in the hip pocket.

In Tia's case, luck appeared in the unlikely shape of Mr Yokomoto's Board of Education minibus, which turned the corner at the end of the street at almost the precise instant that Gannon's Citroën zoomed past it. Tia saw its usefulness in a flash – although the Earthquakes weren't quite as happy about it.

Yoyo's hair practically stood on end along with his vehicle, as Tia de-energized the engine, bringing it to a sudden, screeching standstill in front of the museum. 'C'mon,' she said sharply, and headed down the steps, beckoning for the boys to follow her.

'You crazy?' called Rocky, hesitating. Asking the Earthquakes to run towards a truant officer was like asking a mouse to run towards a cat. 'We don't wanna go to school!' said Crusher horrified.

Tia turned. She could see by the bewildered expressions that the Earthquakes thought she had gone bananas. And she couldn't blame them. 'Trust me,' she appealed urgently, 'please trust me.'

Dazzler shrugged. Tia hadn't let them down so far, why should she now? It looked crazy, sure, but then everything Tia was involved in seemed crazy. He started down the steps, and the others fell in behind him.

Tia smiled. She tugged back the door of the minibus and the gang hopped in. Yoyo was sitting motionless at the wheel. His pouchy face was popeyed and incredulous. 'I'm dreaming,' he mused, as the youngsters filed past him towards the seats. 'Are you kids surrendering to the Board of Education?'

Nobody said anything. Tia didn't want to spoil Yoyo's dream, so she said: 'Mr Yokomoto – see that car going down the street? My brother's in it, and he ought to be in school, too. You should catch up with him.'

Yoyo's face lit up. 'Another truant?' he beamed, hardly able to believe his ears. 'Whatta load this'll be!' He reached forward and turned on the engine. He began to turn the wheel to bring the minibus around in a U turn.

Tia, however, knew a quicker way to get started. Before Yoyo had even started to move off, she had taken control of the minibus. Energized, the vehicle suddenly span round on its own axis to face in the other direction. Roaring like an unleashed tiger, it hurtled off down the street after the Citroën, with Yoyo clinging to the steering wheel for dear life. 'Hey – what's going on?' he protested. Behind him, the Earthquakes exchanged knowing glances. They knew now that Yoyo's minibus wouldn't be going anywhere near the school – at least not while Tia was intent on catching her brother.

The bus was moving at tremendous speed. Whole blocks flashed by in a blur of concrete and glass. In no time at all they were drawing close enough to their quarry to make out the licence plates. Even Yoyo was starting to enjoy the ride. Somehow, he had convinced himself that he was back in command of the minibus, and was bent over the wheel like a maniac, eyes bright with exhilaration. 'Hey, this thing can really move,' he said with pride in his voice. The youngsters grinned. They were pleased to see that even an old sour-puss like Yoyo could get carried away once in a while.

But Yoyo's heady enjoyment was about to be rudely curtailed. Up ahead in the Citroën, Gannon had turned Tony's head so that he could see their pursuers. 'That minibus is chasing us,' he said evenly. 'I command you to place obstacles in its path.'

There was no time for Yoyo to take evasive action. As the Citroën roared past a building site, a bare three seconds ahead of the minibus, a large, very solid-looking cement truck glided out from its parking space to interpose itself between pursuer and pursued. The Earthquakes yelled and dived for cover behind the seats as they saw the cement truck come to a halt broadside across the road. There was no way Yoyo could stop the minibus in time; a collision was inevitable. Then, at the last moment, Tia averted disaster. The steering wheel span out of Yoyo's grasp and the minibus swerved violently, bouncing up on to the sidewalk. But Tia had been a split second too slow and the near offside end of the bus slammed into the cement truck with a bone-jarring crunch. There was a sound of rending metal and a long, jagged hole was torn in the minibus' bodywork. Fortunately though, the angle of impact had been shallow and the bus powered on through the gap and bumped back down on to the tarmac, rejoining the chase. It sped away up the street.

Yoyo let out a long, agonized moan. 'City property!' he wailed. 'I've damaged City property!' He looked as if he were about to cry.

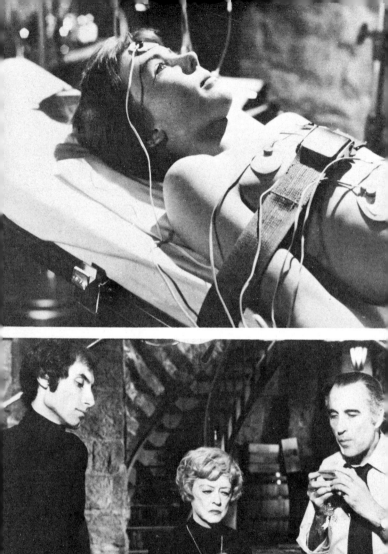

The Earthquakes poked their heads cautiously over the back of the seats. They couldn't believe it. Somehow, they were all still in one piece. But they had little time in which to celebrate their survival, for up ahead Tony was placing yet another obstacle in their path. Suddenly, they all went very white and ducked down again.

'Oh no...' said Yoyo pleadingly. He watched in horror as a fifty-foot long school bus swung out from the kerb, to stretch across the width of the road. This time it would be impossible to swerve around, for there were vehicles parked bumper-to-bumper along both sides of the road. This was it, thought Yoyo. How ironic that it should be a school bus which was going to end his career! He covered his face with his arms, and waited for the impact.

It didn't come. Two seconds dragged by that seemed like an eternity. Then Yoyo opened his eyes again. The bus had vanished! But wait ... where had that long black shadow appeared from? He cast his eyes upwards. He half-knew already what he was going to see, but that didn't make it any easier to believe. Yes. There it was! A flying school bus! He craned his neck up and around as they shot underneath it and watched in amazement as the big vehicle descended gently back to earth behind them.

The Earthquakes resurfaced and let out a wild cheer. 'Atta girl, Tia!' yelled Crusher.

Yoyo looked dazed and pale. 'Was that a bus or a bridge?' he asked vacantly. But Tia didn't have time for explanations; it was doubtful whether Yoyo would have believed the truth anyway. The chase was on again, hotter than ever. Up ahead, Sickle was using some tactics of his own, trying to shake the pursuers by taking a series of sharp tyre-squealing turns through the sidestreets. But the minibus held on doggedly, slicing corners very fine to stay in touch with its more manoeuvrable quarry.

All too often this produced a heart-stopping moment of near-collision with some innocent vehicle, but each time Tia managed to swing safely clear. Behind them, the chasing cars left a trail of black skid-marks and blaring horns.

In spite of everything, the hound remained glued to the weaving hare. Five long minutes and much scorched rubber later, the two vehicles were running down a shallow slope towards the city railroad depot. Tia saw the Citroën's brake-lights flicker momentarily as it whipped into a vicious left-hand turn that would take it across the double line of railroad tracks and on into the western half of town. She brought the minibus around in a similarly tight fashion, and heard the Earthquakes howl as they were thrown around behind her. Two hundred yards ahead, the Citroën was approaching the tracks. Tia expected to see it slow a little to negotiate them, but it didn't. Then she saw why. Lumbering down the line, clanking and rattling, came a long freight train. It sounded a deep-throated blast on its hooter as the Citroën shuddered across the tracks, scant yards ahead of it.

Yoyo swallowed hard. Turning to Tia, he said, 'That brother of yours ... he really doesn't want to go to school, does he? Maybe we better let him get away, mmmn?' He tried jamming his foot down on the brakes, but to no effect. Tia was in complete control of the minibus as it hurtled towards the long ribbon of goods trucks. The Earthquakes wondered what was going through her mind. Surely even Tia's powers would not be enough to levitate a whole train? They weren't, and she knew it. But her face remained calm and concentrated. She knew exactly what to do.

Accordingly, twenty-five yards before impact, the minibus became airborne. It came off the tarmac perfectly, nose first, soared in a graceful arc above the line of trucks, and descended to a sweet four-point touchdown on the other side. Beautiful. The flight had been as smooth as a ski-jump, and Tia's face was a picture of calm confidence.

'Wow,' gasped Dazzler, 'if I'd known I was gonna fly today, I'd have brought along my parachute.'

Yoyo had gone past the point of despair and had been reduced to a state of gibbering astonishment. 'We flew,' he muttered to himself in a voice stretched thin as fuse wire. 'We flew, we flew!'

'They flew,' echoed Gannon, looking back from the rear of the speeding Citroën. He was thunderstruck, but couldn't help being impressed. Tony's sister had overcome every obstacle placed in her way. She was clearly every bit as powerful – and as clever – as her brother. Gannon's mouth set in a hard line. His blocking tactics had proved ineffective. Very well. He must try a different stratagem. He must try to out-think his young adversary.

The Citroën was approaching the brow of a hill. 'Sickle,' rapped Gannon, 'stop the car as soon as we are over the top.'

Letha twisted round, looking worried. 'I hope you don't intend for us to do any flying,' she said.

Gannon ignored her. The car breasted the hill and Sickle jammed on the brakes, bringing the vehicle to a sliding halt against the kerb, a little way down the slope. 'Tony,' continued Gannon determinedly, 'you will cause the reflection of the sun on the rear window to magnify and shine so brightly that our pursuers will be blinded by it.'

Tia had no idea what had happened. For that matter neither did anyone else in the minibus. Three seconds after they had seen the Citroën dip out of sight, they came powering over the brow of the hill. The rear window of the Citroën, angled perfectly, exploded with an intense white light so brilliant that it almost threw Tia out of her seat. It was as if they had driven into the noiseless flash of a gigantic flashbulb. The searing light filled the windshield, blotting everything from view. Yoyo and the Earthquakes yelled in anguish and threw their hands up to shield their eyes. 'Turn it off, Tia!' shouted Muscles.

But Gannon's ruse had served its purpose. Before Tia could recover, the minibus had slewed across the street, hopelessly out of control. Still clocking fifty miles per hour, it slammed into the side of a parked truck and careered off again, back into the centre of the road. Tia saw the world tilt crazily as the minibus rolled over on to its roof. The engine shrieked. There was a wild tangle of arms and legs and loose objects. Screeching horribly, the vehicle began to slide away down the steep hill, scudding past the stationary Citroën. Tia tumbled awkwardly and banged her head on something hard. Dazed and disorientated, she was unable to use her energizing powers, and the minibus slithered on, gradually picking up speed.

Yoyo and the Earthquakes were tossed about like rag dolls. They grabbed wildly for something to hang on to as the world flashed by upside down. Once or twice, the minibus struck the kerb and bounced off, sending itself into a half spin that dislodged any holds its passengers had managed to find. It flashed through an intersection, narrowly missing an ice-cream van and practically giving its driver heart failure.

The hill seemed to go on for ever. Down and down slid the minibus. Eventually, after what seemed an age to Tia and her companions, the slope began to flatten out. Then there was a sharp curve to the left and it was at this point that the minibus parted with the road for the final time. It hit the kerb three-quarters on and bounced up on to the sidewalk, scything a water hydrant from its base, and ploughing on into a fifteen-foot-high wire fence that formed the perimeter of a children's playground. A powerful column of water jetted into the air from the severed hydrant.

The fencing provided an excellent safety net. It stretched and buckled under the force of the impact, but was strong enough to prevent the minibus from bursting through. There was a wrenching, tearing sound and then stillness. The two rear wheels of the minibus were still turning. From inside the hood there came the slow gurgle of escaping liquids.

For a moment nothing moved. Then slowly, one of the side doors creaked open and a figure tumbled dizzily out. It was Yoyo. He turned and reached back inside to give the youngsters a helping hand. One by one they staggered out. It seemed that, apart from being bruised and badly shaken, they were all miraculously unharmed.

Yoyo took a step backwards to review his beloved minibus. It was a write-off. 'Look what's happened to City property,' he groaned, clamping a hand to his head. The minibus was the Board of Education's newest vehicle – a mere two months old. Now it was a heap of junk. What was Yoyo going to tell them? The thought of his embarrassed explanations made him groan even louder.

He shook his head. At least, he supposed, the day hadn't been a total loss. 'Since you kids,' he said, 'have agreed to go back to school, then maybe they'll let me . . .' His voice trailed off as he looked around. Tia and the Earthquakes were gone. He sprinted round to the far side of the minibus, but they weren't there either. Turning, he was just in time to see the last of them speeding around the corner at the far end of the street.

This just wasn't Yoyo's day.

7 The Trap

That night, back at the hideout, Tia lay alone on her bed turning the events of the day over in her mind.

Despite all her efforts she was no nearer to being reunited with her brother. Worse still, she now knew that he had fallen under the influence of some evil partnership, and that he was being used to further their criminal interests. It explained a lot of things. It was clear now, for instance, why Tony hadn't made contact with her in the normal way. Quite simply, he couldn't. The villainous-looking woman and her accomplices had such a powerful hold over Tony that he was incapable of sending anything but garbled telepathic messages. Indeed, remembering back to the museum, it seemed he even had trouble recognizing his own sister! Tia shuddered as she recalled the vacant soulless look that had been in Tony's eyes. What was it that had put it there? Had he been drugged? And what was that strange electronic gadget that the woman had been carrying? Did that have something to do with Tony's condition? There were so many questions, and so few answers. Come tomorrow, she must try and come up with some. There was one slight lead – the big black limousine. With its darkened windows, it was the kind of car which would be recognized anywhere, and there was always the chance that one of the Earthquakes' friends might know where it belonged.

Tia yawned. She had expended a lot of energy

today, both physical and mental, yet still her brain reeled with tortured thoughts of her brother. Finally, however, tiredness won and she dropped off into a shallow, fitfull sleep.

Yet even sleep held no comfort for her. Jumbled images flooded her mind. Events of the past few days flashed in and out of focus in a strange, disjointed order. She tossed restlessly. There was a voice, a clear insistent whisper which echoed through her dream. It kept repeating her name, over and over again. *'Tia,'* it said softly, *'Tia , Tia, Tia ...'* Once or twice, it faded away, only to return again stronger and more urgently than before.

Tia awoke with a start. She put a hand to her forehead, and felt it damp with perspiration. Perhaps, she thought, a drink might help her to sleep. She swung her legs to the floor and got up. There was a carton of milk on the table and she went to get it.

'Tia,' said the voice.

She froze. The word rang through her mind like a pistol shot. So it was real! Tony was trying to communicate with her. She closed her eyes and concentrated, but there were no images coming through. Her mind was blank.

'Tia,' came the voice again a second later.

'I'm here, Tony,' transmitted Tia excitedly.

'Tia, listen carefully. Follow my voice. It will lead you to me.'

Tia's heart lifted. In the midst of his difficulties, Tony had found a way to make contact. Now he wanted her to trace him, to 'home-in' on his telepathic signal. It was a device they had used many times before and – within an operational range of about five miles – it usually had a high rate of success.

Tia dressed hurriedly and went down stairs. Outside, the moon hung over the rooftops like a large white balloon, and the night air was cool on her face.

'Tia,' said Tony again, and she turned to her left, automatically locking-on to the direction of the signal's source. She set off across the city at a brisk walk. Slowly, inexorably, she was wound in towards her brother like a fish on the end of a line. But it was a tricky operation. Here and there the line would get snagged. Tia would falter at an intersection, not sure of which street to take. But always Tony's voice would whisper again in her head and guide her back in the right direction.

It took her a full hour. Tia had covered the better part of three miles by the time she approached the large imposing residence that stood on a hillside on the city outskirts. Rising up from the darkness, it looked more like a fortress than a house, hewn as it was from natural grey stone and surrounded by a high, thick wall. Tia knew her journey was over. Tony was somewhere inside this house, waiting for her. She must be careful how she approached, for she fancied the occupants might not be too pleased to see her.

She pushed at the big wrought-iron gates and they creaked open, allowing her into the driveway. Her feet crunched on the gravel. It was only twenty yards or so to the front door. So far, so good. As she drew nearer, Tony's voice came to her again.

'Tia — where are you?'

'Outside the house.'

'Try and find a way in. I'm in the basement.'

'Okay.'

Predictably, the front door was locked. Tia edged around the porch. She was in luck: someone had left open the sliding glass doors which led out on to the rear patio. She slipped inside.

The room was very large and the bright moonlight cast irregular patterns on the walls. Tia found a door and, holding her breath, eased it open. A moment later, she found herself standing in a wide, finely-decorated hall. A staircase rose away into the darkness. Beneath it, on the wall, a narrow strip of yellow light attracted her attention. She moved closer. It was a half-opened door, of a kind which was designed to close flush with the wood-panelling. Tia eased her way through and came to a sudden halt – she had almost fallen down the flight of stone steps that were on the other side. Her mind raced: she had found the basement. The lights were on, but there was no one to be seen. Down below, she could see the laboratory and the operating table and she realized at once that this was the place she had mistaken for a hospital.

She came quietly down the steps, eyes scanning the layout of the laboratory. There were several doors leading off it and she moved across to try one. She froze in mid-stride. There had been a movement somewhere off to the right. She turned, prepared for the worst. Then her lips parted in a relieved smile – it had only been the laboratory goat shuffling around in his cage. Tia shrugged mentally and returned to the business in hand.

She tried three doors. The first led into the wine cellar, which was empty. The second opened on to a small storeroom, which again was empty. The third was right.

'Tony!' exclaimed Tia.

Her brother was sitting upright on the end of a narrow bunk bed. He was looking directly towards her, but there was no smile on his face, nor any gleam of welcome in his eyes. Tia came forward to reach out a hand. 'Tony,' she repeated, worriedly. But there was no reply.

Everything happened so quickly that Tia barely had time to let out a squeal of surprise. As she stepped into the room, a pair of bony arms – Sickle's – reached out and grabbed her from behind. At the same instant, Letha appeared from out of the shadows and began tugging roughly at the sleeve of her jacket. Then Gannon's hard face loomed towards her and, too late, she saw the hypodermic needle in his right hand. It jabbed downwards.

Tony's empty, impassive gaze, was the last thing Tia remembered as the room tilted and she tumbled down into the deep black pool of unconsciousness.

The trap had worked perfectly.

Gannon had made his decision to capture Tia for two reasons. Firstly, she posed a threat to his plans. Her attempt to rescue Tony at the museum showed that she would stop at nothing to help her brother, and that could prove to be a nuisance, for she was bound to try again. Therefore, reasoned Gannon, it would be better to have her where he could be sure she would cause no further trouble.

Secondly, and perhaps more importantly, Tia could eventually be as useful to him as Tony. Two children with the ability to energize matter were, after all, better than one. That idea would have to wait however, until he had constructed a duplicate of his mind-control device. Meanwhile, Tia must be kept sedated, lest she cause any more problems. And that wasn't an easy task. Administering knock-out injections every few hours would be impractical. Something more permanent – and reliable – would have to be arranged.

By morning, he had the solution. Rushing down to the laboratory, he began to put his idea into practice. Half an hour later, he had constructed a long, transparent casing made from sections of tubular-steel and plastic sheeting. Carrying it to the operating table, he lowered it gently down over Tia's sleeping form. Then he spent some time making sure of an airtight seal between the table's edge and the casing. When this was done, Tia was encased in a transparent module, the atmosphere of which could be controlled at Gannon's will. A slow trickle of sleep-gas into the module would ensure that Tia was kept harmlessly unconscious. He went to search for a cylinder in the storeroom.

It was at that moment Tia began to struggle back to consciousness. Her eyes flickered, and the laboratory swam in and out of focus. The injection she had been given last night was very potent, but gradually her extraordinary willpower helped her to surface. She tried to consider her plight. She was pinned to the operating table and covered by some kind of plastic cover. And judging by the sounds coming from the storeroom she was not alone.

Her first thoughts were to break free and make a run for it, but when she tried to energize the leather straps nothing happened. Slowly she realized that the effect of the injection had weakened her considerably, and it was difficult to raise a finger, let alone use her energizing powers. Even if she did break free, she wasn't sure she could fight her way out, at least not in her present dazed condition. She tried to think of something else. She raised her head a little and let her eyes roam around the laboratory.

That was when she saw Alfred. Alfred the billy-goat was kneeling on a bed of straw in his cage, enjoying a peaceful doze. The only thoughts in his head were of lazy, hot days and endless fields of lush green grass. Tia was about to change all that. Summoning up the little strength she possessed, she projected her weakened mental power across the laboratory and lifted the tiny latch on the door of Alfred's cage. Next second Alfred's eyes popped wide open. Suddenly, his clouded brain was imbued with a sense of urgency — and purpose. He didn't know why, but he knew he had a task to perform, and that he must perform it as quickly as possible.

Tia smiled as she saw, with some relief, that her message had been received and was about to be acted upon. As she watched, Alfred jerked to his feet and nosed open the cage door. He skipped lightly across the stone flagging, and then with a reassuring glance at Tia, clopped on up the steps and through the narrow doorway at the top.

A second later, Gannon came back into the laboratory, dragging a cylinder of sleep-gas behind him. Tia closed her eyes and prayed he wouldn't notice the empty cage. But he was too wrapped up with his own scheming thoughts. He clipped the cylinder into place and rotated the tiny metal wheel. The gas hissed into the plastic casing. Another second and Tia was drifting helplessly back into unconsciousness. All her hopes were now pinned on Alfred.

He was doing well so far. Neither Letha nor Sickle had noticed him as he passed across the hall and out of the front door. Nor had they seen him as he cantered away down the driveway and out on to the main road. He made good speed down the hill. In only fifteen minutes, he was nearing the city centre. Unfortunately, that was when his troubles began. It was still early morning, and the main streets were clogged with rush-hour traffic – and somehow Alfred had to cross them in order to reach his destination. He paused with both front hoofs on the kerb, inclining his head and looking puzzled. The cars were jammed nose to bumper along the length of the street, waiting for the lights.

Alfred decided to negotiate the traffic the only way he knew how: over the top. There was a dull metallic thud as he leapt up on to the trunk of the nearest car and began his progress across to the far side of the street.

One well-heeled lady driver was taking advantage of the hold-up to apply some lipstick. Suddenly, there was a thump on the car roof, and the next moment she was staring at the upside down, inquisitive head of a billy-goat. She shrieked and jerked back, and the red lipstick described a vertical line up the middle of her face.

Alfred couldn't understand what all the fuss was about. He snorted and jumped on to the hood of the next car, the driver of which was in the act of lighting a cigarette for his lady companion. Both of them looked up as Alfred's hooves clattered on the bodywork. Their mouths dropped open. The woman's cigarette fell from her mouth and the man's lighter ignited the big feather in her hat. He turned just in time to see what he had done. Snatching the hat, he leapt out of the car, threw it on the ground and began jumping up and down on it.

Alfred was quite bemused by these strange antics, and he simply chose to ignore them, leap-frogging on across the packed ranks of automobiles. Behind him, he left a trail of shocked faces, raised voices, and dented car bodywork.

*

About the same time, a few miles north of the city, Gannon's black Citroën pulled smoothly to a halt on a lonely stretch of country road. Sickle got out smartly and opened the doors for Gannon, Letha and Tony. Together, the four of them moved across to the edge of the road. They found themselves standing on a hilltop which had a commanding view of the surrounding country. The great green and brown carpet of landscape lay stretched out before them, latticed by straight grey ribbons of road and the occasional twist of a river.

Directly below, nestled in the palm of a narrow valley, lay a sprawling factory complex. A high perimeter fence formed a rectangle around the blocks of concrete buildings which were connected to each other by flat thoroughfares. Near the centre of the complex, projecting from the ground like a massive wart, was a shining white sphere, some two hundred and fifty feet in diameter.

'What kind of factory is that?' queried Sickle.

'It's a plutonium processing plant, where U-235 becomes U-239,' explained Gannon, the facts at his fingertips.

'Translate that into financial terms,' requested Letha.

Gannon smirked. 'Plutonium is more valuable than gold,' he said.

Letha's eyes gleamed. 'That's what I like about science,' she said. 'They're always discovering more expensive things.'

'What's so good about plutonium?' Sickle was being his usual sceptical self.

'It's used as the explosive core of nuclear warheads,' answered Gannon patiently. 'If that's what you call good.'

'And I suppose you'll have Tony whip up an atom bomb or something?' joked Letha. She began a cackling little laugh, but it faded abruptly as she saw the serious expression on Gannon's face. She flicked a nervous glance at Sickle.

'Plutonium,' continued Gannon stonily, 'is the most powerful radioactive element of all. We will take over the atomic furnace where it is processed, cause a chain reaction explosion, and release a radioactive cloud that will drift from city to city.'

'I didn't count on killing anyone,' said Letha worriedly. 'Especially not us.'

Gannon smiled as though talking to a child. 'It'll never go that far,' he assured her. 'They'll pay anything to prevent it. Do you think that five million dollars might spread some joy among your accountants?'

Letha felt a warm glow rising inside her. Now her partner was talking a language she could understand. 'It'll blow the transistors clear out of their calculators,' she beamed.

Gannon took a deep breath and cast his eye over the landscape. 'This is the first step,' he proclaimed, 'in making myself the most powerful man in the world.' Then, turning on his heel, he led the assembled company back to the car. Doors slammed shut, Sickle switched on and they moved off down the hillside towards the floor of the valley.

Within five minutes they had arrived at the entrance to the plutonium plant. There was a small gatehouse containing a uniformed guard who controlled two automatic lifting barriers which served the narrow entrance and exit lanes. As the Citroën approached, a truck drew up behind the exit barrier, its radio tuned-in loudly to a country and western station. The guard leaned out to check the driver's papers and, satisfied with them, waved him through. The gate swung up and the truck moved off. Sickle wound down his window as the guard turned to deal with the Citroën.

'What can I do for you folks?'

Letha leaned across from the passenger's seat. 'You can take a powder,' she said sweetly.

The guard frowned momentarily, which was about all he had time to do.

Next moment, his entire gatehouse was lifting straight up into the air, swing barriers and all. Like some strange metal and glass bird, borne aloft on spindly wings, it flew after the departing truck and landed neatly on the tailboard. 'Get me outta here!' yelled the guard, struggling feverishly with the gatehouse door. 'Help!' But the truck driver drove nonchalantly on, deaf to everything except the wail of country and western guitars that issued forth from his radio.

Gannon smiled with satisfaction and ordered Sickle to drive on. As they entered the grounds of the plant, he pointed towards a tall, pylon-like metal tower which stood a short distance away to their right. 'Tony,' he ordered, 'that is the outer security scanner. Put it out of commission.'

There was no explosion, but the scanner toppled over as if it had been dynamited. With a rending screech, it fell forwards and collapsed into a twisted mass of mangled girders. Some distance away, in the security control block, a guard leapt out of his seat as the bank of video monitors on the wall before him suddenly went dead. 'Hey – what's going on?' he said nervously, reaching out to stab wildly at a panel of buttons. 'What's happened?'

Outside, the Citroën raced on, with Gannon shouting directions from the back seat. Two minutes and three sharp, right-angled turns later, the black limousine slithered to a halt beside the big white metal dome, at the hub of the complex: the furnace building. The group jumped out and clattered down a metal stairway towards the main door. A second before they reached it, the door began to swing open and there was just time for them to flatten against the curving wall before being seen. Three guards, alerted by their colleagues at security control, came rushing out and bounded up the stairway.

Unnoticed, the four intruders slipped quickly into the building. Gannon's eyes glowed with the dark fire of determination. Once inside the furnace room itself, he would have the world in the palm of his hands. Nothing and no one could stop him now.

8 The Rescue

Alfred saw his chance.

The cab was pointed towards the south side of the city, and that was the way he had to go. Of course, there was no guarantee it would take him in the right direction, but he was tired now, and anyway it was worth a try. He had seen a man hail the cab and now he watched as it pulled over and the driver stuck his craggy face out of the window.

'Where to, mister?'

'Fourth and Market.'

'Hop in.'

The man opened the back door and started to get in. That was when Alfred made his move. He charged forward, head dipping low, and the poor, unsuspecting fare never knew what hit him. Alfred's stubby horns connected solidly with the seat of his trousers and he went sailing across the width of the car, crashing heavily into the far door. He fell on the inset handle and the door swung open, toppling him out on to the street.

Alfred clambered in and parked himself on the back seat. The whole switch had taken place in less than five seconds. The cab driver slammed the flag down and reached a hand behind him to close the rear door. Then he jabbed the accelerator and moved out into the stream of traffic. Back on the street, his would-be passenger picked his bruised body off the tarmac and waved his arms in consternation.

Alfred had been luckier than he could have imagined. Not only had he managed to get a cab all to himself – he had chosen the fastest cab-driver in the city to ferry him: none other than the free-wheeling tyre-squealing Eddie. 'Have you there in a coupla minutes, mister,' he shouted over his shoulder.

'Baaaaa ...' said Alfred.

'Yes, sir,' continued Eddie, accelerating hard down the outside of a line of slow-moving traffic. 'Feel the power in this cab? It's got plenty of power. Everybody tells me I oughtta be a race driver. What do you think?'

'Baaaaa ...'

'Well, I think you're wrong!' Eddie stomped on the brake pedal and tried to squeeze into a gap hardly big enough for a push bike. Horns blared. 'I'll tell yar this,' said Eddie with confidence, 'I'm a real safe driver. I been hackin' nineteen years eleven months. In all that time I never even scratched a cab. Next month they're gonna give me a gold safety award. What do you think of that?'

'Baaaaa ...'

'Ah, you don't like nothin'. I sure hope you're a good tipper.'

'Baaaaa ...'

'Huh. I didn't think you were.' Eddie shrugged and swung left on to a sidestreet, hoping to lose some of the heavy morning traffic. His eyes flickered over the rear-view mirror. At first, nothing registered. Then disbelievingly, he grabbed for a rag in the glove-box and wiped it over the mirror. Then he looked again. Alfred's face was still there, staring benignly back at him 'Baaaaa ...' said Alfred.

Eddie's mouth sagged open and he span round, still not believing the evidence of the mirror. But it was true. There was a fully grown free-loading billy-goat seated in the back of his cab!

Eddie didn't have much time to puzzle over how it

got there. Next instant, he was jerked violently back towards the windshield as his swerving cab slammed into the rear of a parked vehicle. There was the sound of breaking glass, a five-yard shunt, and then both cars came to a standstill.

Eddie winced, switched off his engine and leapt out. Furiously, he yanked open the back door. 'Get outta my cab!' he yelled. 'Out! Out!'

Alfred had the feeling he wasn't wanted any more. Sheepishly, he clambered out of the cab and set off up the street at a steady trot. Eddie watched him disappear around the corner and then, with heart in mouth, turned to inspect the damage to his beloved cab. 'My perfect record,' he moaned, tears welling in his eyes. 'My perfect record.'

It wasn't until he looked up from the battered hood of his vehicle, more than a minute later, that he noticed the distinctive blue and white colouring on the car he had driven into. By that time, its driver – a patrolman – was standing over him with an expression of barely restrained fury on his face, waiting for an explanation.

Eddie cleared his throat nervously. 'I picked up this guy three blocks away,' he began brokenly, 'and next thing I know, it ain't a guy anymore – it's a goat! And then I . . .'

'Don't tell me,' interrupted the patrolman, reaching for his pocketbook. 'Let me guess. When you asked for a tip, the goat sprouted wings and flew away. Right?'

Luckily, the Earthquakes were still at the hideout when Alfred showed up. There had been no trace of Tia when they arrived with her breakfast that morning, save for her discarded red waistcoat which hung limply over the back of a chair. Neither had there been any note to explain her sudden disappearance. The

Earthquakes were baffled. There was nothing they could do, they concluded, except to wait and hope that she would turn up again.

Their vigil had not been without its compensations however, for Muscles had brought along a big bag of hotcakes, and as the gang quickly discovered they were the most delicious thing this side of a multi-layered ice-cream sundae.

'When we run away from home,' said Crusher wistfully, 'I'm sure gonna miss your mom's hotcakes, Muscles.'

Rocky murmured his agreement. A guy certainly had to make a lot of sacrifices if he wanted to be tough and independent. 'It's too bad,' added Dazzler, through a mouthful of hotcake, 'that Tia isn't here to ...' his voice trailed off, as there came a scuffling sound from the other side of the door. 'Hey – that must be her now,' said Rocky, and bounded across to open the door. When he jerked it open however, he got the shock of his life. It was not Tia who confronted him, but a determined billy-goat named Alfred. 'Look out!' shouted Rocky, nearly jumping out of his skin.

He raced back into the room and clambered on to the table, as Alfred came charging towards him, bleating and snorting. The rest of the gang jumped on the nearest piece of furniture they could find.

'It's a wild beast!' yelled Crusher.

'Oh, Tia ... where are you when we need you?' moaned Muscles, balancing precariously on the window ledge.

Alfred scraped the floorboards with his front hoof and scampered excitedly about the room, knocking chairs over and nuzzling each of the Earthquakes in turn. Eventually, he came to a halt beneath Dazzler, who had leapt to the sanctuary of the bunk bed. He lifted both hooves on to the edge of the bed and pressed his nose against Dazzler's legs. 'Hey – it's actin' like it knows me!' said Dazzler nervously.

'Baaaaa ...' answered Alfred, nudging him.

'What do you want from me?'

'Baaaaa ...' repeated Alfred and trotted off towards the door. He paused there for a moment, then turned and trotted back again.

'Maybe he's hungry,' suggested Rocky.

'Watch out – don't let him get the hotcakes,' said Muscles fearfully, as he saw Alfred move towards the table. But the warning was misapplied. Instead of going for the bag of goodies, Alfred ducked his nose towards the back of a fallen chair and, snatching Tia's red waistcoat in his mouth, made hurriedly for the door. 'Hey – come back here!' shouted Dazzler.

All fear temporarily forgotten, the Earthquakes leapt down from their perches and gave chase. The situation had taken on a new turn: breaking up the furniture was one thing, but stealing Tia's clothing was quite another. Alfred clomped heavily down the staircase and the Earthquakes tumbled clumsily after him.

It was exactly what Alfred wanted. Now that he had the Earthquakes in tow, he wasn't about to let them off the hook. It was important not to let them catch him, but it was equally important that he should not get too far ahead, lest they should lose interest in the chase. Alfred played it perfectly. The hectic pursuit took them back into town, past the startled gazes of drivers and pedestrians alike, and out again towards the eastern suburbs.

This time, however, there were no taxi rides and the journey took them over half an hour to complete. It was mid-morning by the time Alfred came crunching up the drive towards Letha's house, still clutching the waistcoat tightly between his teeth. A few yards behind him, the Earthquakes came puffing and panting along, all but exhausted by their long run up the hill. But they weren't giving up now: Alfred seemed to be running himself into a corner. Tia's waistcoat was not yet lost.

Alfred skirted the front and side of the house and finally found his way through the half-open patio doors. He led his boisterous pursuers scuttling through the lounge and out into the hall. Then he paused, for the panelled door leading to the basement was closed. Well, what was the point of having horns if you didn't use them? Head down, Alfred took a short powerful little run at the door and smashed a jagged hole in it, jumping through and bounding down the steps on the far side. The Earthquakes squeezed after him.

Dazzler came to a stumbling halt halfway down the stone staircase and held up his hand to stop the others. 'Hey, look!' he shouted, and suddenly all thoughts about Alfred were forgotten.

'It's Tia!' yelled Rocky.

The Earthquakes gasped in surprise. Excitedly, they leapt down the remaining few steps and rushed across to the operating table. 'She's being fed some kinda gas,' said Dazzler. 'Let's get her outta there.' Crusher was way ahead of him. He had already found the outlet tap on the cylinder and turned it off. Meanwhile, the rest of them set about removing the transparent casing. A few seconds later, it was lifted off and eager hands rushed to undo the leather straps that held Tia to the table.

The smell of sleep-gas tainted the air as Tia gradually emerged back into the land of the living. It took her fully two minutes to recognize her rescuers and another three before she had completely recovered. Dazzler fetched a glass of water and held it to Tia's lips as the others helped her to sit up. 'Okay now?' he asked.

'Yes,' said Tia gratefully. 'Thank you.'

'How'd you get here?' Muscles wanted to know.

'It was Tony,' explained Tia, thinking back to the events of the previous night. 'He was calling me . . .' She paused, furrowed her brow, and looked around the laboratory. 'Where is he now?' she asked fearfully.

'You're asking us?' countered Rocky.

Tia brushed her friends aside, slid down from the table and started across the laboratory towards the room where she had last seen her brother. She had taken only three strides, however, when she stopped dead in her tracks. 'I saw something!' she cried, face screwed tight in concentration.

'What was it?' chorused the Earthquakes, rushing across to her side.

Tia looked as if she were in agony, straining to make sense of the hazy telepathic signal which had flashed into her mind. 'It's a big, round . . . thing!' she said brokenly. 'That's where Tony is. I'm sure of it. Big, round . . . and white . . .'

Crusher had the answer. 'Like a ball?' he asked. 'Like a great big ball?'

'Yes!'

'I know where it is!'

Tia almost exploded with anxiety. 'Let's go then!' she said. 'Hurry!' She bounded across to the stairway and started up the steps two at a time, with the Earthquakes right behind her. They were almost all through the shattered doorway at the top when Tia realized there was something she had forgotten to do. She checked, turned and ran back down to the laboratory.

'Thank you for everything,' she murmured, reaching her arms around Alfred's neck to give him a big, warm hug.

'Baaaaa ...' said Alfred modestly.

Tia smiled. Alfred had performed wonderfully, and she would never forget him. She patted him once, kissed him, and took off up the steps again. Behind her, Alfred snorted with pride and pushed his nose back into a much-deserved bowl of feed.

Gannon and his entourage had almost reached the furnace room. Their footsteps echoed off the metal walls as they headed towards the massive steel door at the end of the corridor. A solitary uniformed guard, seated at a desk, was all the human resistance they had left to overcome.

'Wait a minute.' The guard rose to his feet as the motley group of intruders approached and came to a halt. His name – Dolan – was printed across a card on his left chestpocket. 'You can't go beyond this point without ID.' The voice was firm, authoritative. He was stating a rule.

Gannon was unperturbed. He produced the control unit. 'Show him our ID, Tony,' he said smiling nonchalantly at the guard.

Dolan reached out a hand, but he didn't get the usual plastic card with an official stamp on it. Instead, he got a magic elevator ride, straight up to the ceiling. Flattened against the metal surface, he looked down with an expression of sheer bewilderment on his moon-like face. 'What's happening?' he babbled. 'What am I doing here ...?'

Ignoring his protests the intruders passed underneath him and came face to face with the giant steel door. There was a sign on it, written in large red letters, which read: 'DANGER: FURNACE ROOM. NO UNAUTHORIZED PERSONNEL.' It looked, Letha fancied, rather like the contraptions found in the depths of bank vaults, and the thought gave her a warm feeling all over.

'Open the door,' commanded Gannon.

Tony complied. The electronic lock was disengaged and the great three-feet-thick steel barrier swung open. It swung back in a gentle arc and allowed the party through. Then Tony closed it again and re-energized the locking device.

This done, the group turned to look around them. They were standing in a massive hall, filled with all kinds of strange apparatus. There were a number of huge, futuristic-looking machines grouped near the centre of the room, wide metal pipes raying out from them in all directions. They were linked to the bulky metal container that lay in the middle: the heart of the furnace itself. Metal staircases wound up and over the machinery and long, spidery catwalks swept around the walls, reaching high up to the great curving bowl of the roof. A deep, persistent humming sound pervaded the whole room.

Gannon led the group along one of the lengthy aisles between the machines, until they arrived at the main control panel. He viewed the dials and switches with an air of confidence. 'We're about to make scientific history,' he proclaimed, an ironic smile tugging at the corners of his mouth.

'And some money, too,' reminded Letha.

Gannon gave her a sideways look and brought Tony forward to face the array of controls. 'Now,' he said, determinedly, 'I want you to shut down the furnace's cooling system – including the emergency backup.'

With android-like precision Tony began work and

91

instantly the low droning hum emitted by the furnace began to change. It was replaced by an ominous wailing sound which slowly began to rise in both pitch and volume...

Up in the main control room, situated at the top of the tall grey block immediately next to the furnace building, the duty monitor's brow creased in a deep frown as he noticed two red warning lights begin to flash on his console. Something was up with the cooling system. He called the operations officer over to take a look. 'Must be a circuit breaker,' came the advice. 'Restart the system.'

The monitor punched up the correct sequence for a restart, but nothing happened. The red lights continued to wink. He cleared the board and tried again. 'I can't get a restart!' he exclaimed anxiously.

The operations officer tried to keep his head. 'Hit the backup system,' he ordered. It was a command which hadn't been heard before in the control room – to date, the backup system had never been required, for the primary one always functioned perfectly. The duty monitor's fingers scrabbled with the lid of the little recessed box which contained the emergency backup button. He flicked it open and stabbed downwards.

'I've got a no-go on the backup!' he said feverishly. The sweat was beginning to collect around his temples.

Then came the predictable call from the cooling system engineer who sat a yard or so to the monitor's right, watching the thermostat indicators. 'Temperature increase in the furnace,' he reported. 'Do something to get that coolant flowing!'

The operations officer hardly needed reminding of his responsibility to act, but for the moment he was stumped. How could both primary and backup systems be out of commission at the same time? The odds against it happening had been computed at a million to one. He moved across to the bank of telephones in order to alert the Director, Clearcole. But before he could do so, the furnace room phone began to ring. He picked it up. The voice on the other end of the line was deep and resonant. 'Control?' it questioned.

'Who is this?'

'My name is Doctor Victor Gannon. I have shut down your cooling system.' The voice sounded unnervingly confident.

'Okay ... if you shut it down ... put it back on.'

'Tell him just how expensive it is to turn it back on,' breathed Letha who was leaning close to the mouthpiece.

'In about an hour,' proceeded Gannon, 'we will be serving grilled plutonium, medium rare, to the atmosphere ... unless the following conditions are met.'

'What conditions?'

'Five million dollars cash ... a jet waiting at the airport, and safe escort. Most important, you will announce that Doctor Victor Gannon has achieved molecular control and mind-control, and that this is the first in a series of worldwide demonstrations of his power. Those wishing to align themselves with me should make their intentions known.'

With that, Gannon replaced the receiver and turned to beam triumphantly at Letha, who was already trying to work out how many suitcases she would need to carry five million dollars. Outside, they heard a siren begin to wail and a steady banging start up behind the furnace door, as the guards tried fruitlessly to break their way in.

9 The Countdown

'There it is!' yelled Crusher at the top of his voice. He was pointing to a huge white golf ball, perched on top of an equally enormous tee, that stood on display outside the entrance to a golf club. A wide self-satisfied smile was stitched across his face.

Tia shook her head disappointedly. 'No,' she sighed, 'that's not it. It was much bigger than that.'

Crusher was crestfallen. He'd been so sure about the big white ball – and now he had been made to look rather foolish. The others began to shove him around for having led them on a wild goose chase. 'Aw, leave me alone willya?' he protested. 'I was only tryin'!'

Disillusioned, they all moved back down the street, trying to think of other locations that might fit the description Tia had given them. But 'big, white, round things' (excluding the moon) didn't come readily to mind. They were all still lost in thought as they rounded the corner and as a result, they practically walked straight into the arms of their most dreaded enemy. Fortunately, Rocky noticed Yoyo just in time. 'Hey – let's get outta here, you guys,' he said anxiously, turning to make a run for it.

But the Earthquakes quickly saw that there was no reason to panic. The legendary Yoyo, scourge of the city's truants, appeared not the least interested. In fact, he waved them away. He was standing hands thrust in pockets, outside the entrance to an auto wrecking yard, surveying the battered remains of his minibus, parked unceremoniously by the kerb. His normally sad face looked more doleful than ever. As the gang watched, he climbed up into the cab and began collecting together his personal items and stuffing them into his jacket pockets. The radio, as if in defiance of being scrapped, was blaring out loud rock music. Yoyo thumped it, but it didn't make any difference.

Tia and the Earthquakes approached the minibus warily. 'Whassamatter, Yoyo?' ventured Dazzler. 'Don't you wanna catch us?'

For a moment, Yoyo simply continued collecting his things together. Then he lifted his bony shoulders in a tired shrug and gave the youngsters an abject look. 'It's not my job anymore,' he said flatly. 'They're on their way down here to fire me.' He banged the radio again, but it only got louder. 'All because I was trying to help you kids.'

The Earthquakes felt a sudden surge of guilt. Yoyo wasn't such a bad guy really, and they had never imagined that he would lose his job. In fact, they never thought of Yoyo having a job in the ordinary sense. To them, he was Yoyo the truant catcher: he had chased them ever since they had started school (or rather since they stopped going) and they naturally assumed he always would. If Yoyo wasn't out to catch them any more, then being a truant wasn't going to be half as much fun. Worse still, the Board of Education might give his job to someone who could run a lot faster – and that would be terrible.

'Maybe he's tryin' to use some of that si-cology on us,' whispered Muscles. But he didn't really believe that, and neither did the rest of the gang.

For what seemed a long time, they shuffled around, heads bowed, uncertain how to handle the situation. Finally, Tia spoke up for all of them. 'Mr Yokomoto,' she said sympathetically, 'we're sorry about what happened.'

Yoyo tried to smile graciously, but couldn't manage

it. 'All I ever wanted out of life,' he explained, 'was someday to have all the kids I put back into school come and visit me and say, "Thanks, Mr Yoyo ... er ... Yokomoto. If it wasn't for you making me get an education, I'd be a creep today." That's all I wanted.' He sniffed and went back to rummaging under the dashboard.

The youngsters felt lower than ever. What could they do to make amends? This feeling of guilt was worse even than the thought of going back to school. Well, perhaps not quite that bad ...

Yoyo thumped the radio again, trying to silence the stream of rock music, but to no avail. Then, suddenly, as if in delayed reaction, the music began to fade away. A serious-voiced announcer came on to deliver an urgent news flash.

'... and the danger to the city of radio-active fallout is increasing,' came the taut, even tones. 'Experts are baffled as to how this condition came about ...'

Yoyo scowled and banged the radio again. If it wasn't bad music, it was bad news, he thought to himself. He was about to hit it again, but Tia called to him to stop.

'An official,' continued the announcement, 'describes the atomic furnace controls as seeming to be frozen in position, as if, quote, the molecular flow had been interrupted, unquote ...'

Tia's mind raced. It was Tony's work – it had to be! Some evil scheme was afoot and Tony was being forced to supply the 'mental muscle' to carry it out. But where was he?

The radio droned on: '... that unless the demands of the terrorists are met, the furnace would explode with the force of ten megatons. The plutonium plant is being evacuated and ...'

96

Tia bit her lip. The plutonium plant! Yes, of course. Now the huge white sphere made sense: it must be the furnace building. 'That's where Tony is!' cried Tia. 'We've got to go there!'

The Earthquakes hesitated. The plutonium plant was over five miles away. 'What are we gonna do ... take a bus?' asked Muscles.

Tia shook her head. 'We'll go in this,' she said, placing a hand on the mangled minibus. Yoyo's eyes nearly popped out of his head. Before he could say anything, strange sounds began to issue from beneath the hood. Energized, the starter motor whirred noisily and, with a grinding screech, brought the engine stammering into life. Coughing and wheezing, the minibus began to belch black smoke from its exhaust. The chassis shook violently as the engine picked up.

The Earthquakes let out a wild cheer and piled into the minibus, pushing past a totally bemused Yoyo. They were airborne again, and loving every minute of it. Tia shoved Yoyo across behind the steering wheel and sat down next to him. 'Oh no ...' said Yoyo, remembering back to last time. 'It's happening again ...'

But the anxiety went unheeded. With a little help from Tia, the minibus crunched into gear and jerked fitfully out into the traffic. Engine wailing, it kangaroo-hopped away down the street.

Clearcole, the plant's Director, had no choice. In the past fifteen minutes, since he had arrived in the main control room, he had been on the hot line to both the city Mayor and the President. They were of the same opinion: like it or not, the money would have to be paid. The risk of the furnace exploding and the subsequent dangers of radiation could not be taken.

The control room was a flurry of frenzied activity. Phones jangled, red lights pulsed and engineers rushed madly to and fro. Outside, the sound of raised voices and clattering footsteps informed Clearcole that his evacuation procedures were already under way. Close by, the chief engineer swivelled round on his seat and thrust a finger towards the large temperature meter in front of him. 'Sir,' he reported tersely, 'if the furnace doesn't start cooling soon, the chain reaction will start.'

Clearcole's mouth tightened and he gave a curt nod of acknowledgement. He looked across the room to where a trio of uniformed guards were grouped around a pile of hefty cash boxes. They were still awaiting a further delivery from government vaults, to bring the money up to the demanded amount.

Time was running out. Clearcole simply couldn't stand around and do nothing. Making a sudden decision, he stepped across to the telephones, and picked up the one marked 'Furnace room'.

'Yes?' Gannon's voice was cool and sinister.

'This is Clearcole. The situation is critical. In ten minutes, this place will be a hole in the ground. We now have three and a half million dollars here in the control room. Let's be reasonable. Accept it and turn the cooling system back on.'

Clearcole fancied he heard a scuffle at the other end of the line, and an excited woman's voice saying 'It's a deal!' but then Gannon was back on the line, sounding more determined than ever. 'I don't make compromises,' he said forcibly, and then the phone went dead.

Yoyo's minibus swept into the plutonium plant doing more than ninety miles per hour. The gatehouse and barrier that would normally have been there to stop it were by this time over halfway to the state line on the back of a truck.

The hectic bustle of evacuating personnel made the minibus zigzag madly on its headlong dash towards the furnace. It's tyres shrieked agonizingly as it whipped around a right-angled bend and skidded to a stop outside the big white dome.

Tia and the Earthquakes leapt out and dashed across to the control block with Yoyo puffing along at the rear. Inside, Tia commandeered an elevator and the group shot up towards the control room. The doors slid open to reveal a scene of near-panic, as the engineers struggled to prevent the furnace from over-heating. The dour-faced Clearcole was shouting orders in all directions, racing from one console to the next, sweating profusely. He almost collided with Tia and the Earthquakes as they tumbled out of the elevator. 'Hey,' he called to his chief of security, 'we can't have sightseeing tours at a time like this!'

Tia grabbed his sleeve in desperation. 'Sir,' she explained, 'the people who are trying to destroy the furnace have kidnapped my brother. If I could see him I might be able to stop him.'

Behind her, the Earthquakes lent their noisy support to the idea. Even Yoyo looked encouraging. But Clearcole was a practical, level-headed man. He couldn't see how a young girl like Tia could even begin to help matters. 'It's impossible,' he replied, 'they've sealed the furnace room door somehow.'

'What part of the furnace has to be fixed?' persisted Tia.

'The emergency cooling system.'

'Where is it?'

'Five levels down.'

That was all Tia needed to know. Turning on her

heels, she rushed back to the elevator and jumped in, the Earthquakes just managing to squeeze in behind her as she jabbed the button for the furnace room. Yoyo wasn't so lucky. His short stride brought him to the elevator just in time to have the doors hiss shut in his face. 'Come back!' he shouted, thumping the wall uselessly.

But Tia had no intention of coming back – at least not without her brother. One quick elevator ride later, she and the Earthquakes were pounding along the corridor towards the furnace room. They braked sharply as they came in sight of Dolan, who was still struggling to unglue himself from the ceiling. 'Get me down from here!' he pleaded.

The youngsters were clearly on the right track. Obligingly, Tia energized Dolan and lowered him gently to the floor.

'Thanks,' he said, wiping a relieved hand over his forehead. 'But hang on a minute ... where are you going?'

Tia nodded to the big steel door. 'Oh no,' said Dolan holding out his arms to bar their way. 'You can't go past this point without ID.'

The warning was instantly regretted. As Tia levitated him smoothly back up to the ceiling, he made a mental note to bring along a pair of magnetic boots for his next stint of guard duty.

Smiling, the youngsters passed through unhindered and arrived at the great furnace door. For the second time that day, it was energized and made to swing smoothly open. The gang stepped inside. As the door eased shut behind them, the smiles faded quickly from their eager faces. The air was electric with a sense of impending danger. The struggle for control of the furnace room was on.

10 The Duel

Tia edged cautiously along the narrow catwalk, keeping as low as possible, with the Earthquakes in single file behind her. From here, she reasoned, they would have a better chance of locating the enemy than down amongst the maze of machinery on the furnace-floor. The height might even give them the advantage of surprise, too.

She was right on the first point, at least. Rounding a sharp bend in the catwalk, the five youngsters came to a sudden halt. Tony and his captors were standing some twenty feet below, grouped in front of the furnace-control panel. Tia paused for a moment to marshal her thoughts. There was no hope of a sneak attack as the group was in a relatively open position, at the end of one of the aisles. There was only one thing for it: she must catch her brother's attention and attempt to break through the powerful influence that Gannon held over him.

Rising up, she leant forward over the steel handrail and yelled, 'Tony!' at the top of her voice.

Down below, the four startled figures span around and looked up. Letha gestured in exasperation. 'I knew it!' she groaned. 'She'll spoil everything! I can taste the money! We can't let her take it away from us!'

Tia was more interested in her brother than the money. Apart from sisterly loyalties, Tony would know how to turn the cooling system back on. Tia achieved eye contact with him, and put everything she had into breaking through the invisible barrier that surrounded his mind. Slowly, very slowly, he began to respond. A deep frown appeared on his forehead and his eyes flickered with the ghost of an expression. His mind was in turmoil.

Gannon had seen the danger signals. Ducking out of sight behind the machinery, he whipped the control unit up to his mouth. 'Tony,' he whispered commandingly, 'from this moment on you cannot hear Tia. She cannot break through my control. Acknowledge.'

The deep, will-sapping voice was irresistible. Tony's mind went blank and his face returned to lifelessness. 'Yes, sir,' he responded dutifully.

Gannon bared his teeth in a self-satisfied grin. The first round was his: now to make the best of his advantage. He waved frantically to Letha and Sickle. 'Get those kids!' he ordered, pointing to the stairway.

Letha hesitated. 'But she'll do those molecule things to us!' she complained.

'I'll get her before she has a chance to,' reassured Gannon. 'You get the others.'

Reluctantly, Letha and Sickle started towards the stairs. Directly above them, Tia still fought to free Tony's mind, not realizing that she had already lost the battle. Suddenly, she broke off concentration and turned to Dazzler. 'I can't get through,' she said dejectedly. 'We'll have to find the emergency cooling system switches ourselves.' So saying, she began to run back along the catwalk, searching for the nearest stairway. 'How do you spell "cooling"?' called Dazzler as he chased after her.

There was no time for English lessons. The stairway that the five youngsters chose to go down turned out to be the same one that Letha and Sickle were ascending. They met on a narrow landing in the middle. Sickle tried to sweep Rocky and Crusher up together, but they were a shade too fast for him and ducked beneath his long, bony reach. Letha, less ambitious, made a wild grab for Muscles, but a nicely-timed feint wrong-footed her and she missed her target. The youngsters bounded on down the remaining steps and on to the furnace-room floor.

'Find the emergency switch,' shouted Tia and the group scattered. It was a good move, for not only did it increase the speed of the youngsters' search, it also made them more difficult to catch – as Letha and Sickle were about to find out.

Tia had gone about halfway down one of the central aisles when she slithered to a halt before one of the many control panels that were dotted around the hall. Turning to study it, she failed to notice that Gannon (with Tony in tow) had cut across to intercept her and was eyeing her closely from behind the cover of throbbing machinery. 'Tony,' he hissed, 'we must eliminate Tia. We will cause that mobile utility panel to run her down.' Tony's eyes flicked across to the proposed weapon: a waist-high, box-like piece of equipment mounted on four small wheels. He energized it and it rolled rapidly towards its mark.

Had the mobile unit been without the benefit of rubber wheels, Tia might have heard it coming a second sooner than she did. As it was, she had very little time to react. The unit came trundling towards her, and she tried to sidestep out of the way. When it corrected course back towards her, she realized it was energized. In the nick of time, she brought her own powers to bear and caused it to swerve. It skimmed by her with inches to spare and slammed with explosive force into the steel wall.

Tia was still picking herself up off the floor when Crusher suddenly appeared around the corner and beckoned to her. She followed him as he ran down another of the aisles. When they came to a halt, Crusher pointed to a complex panel of switches and Tia heaved a sigh of relief. He had found the cooling system controls. She closed her eyes and concentrated. Immediately, the circuitry was unjammed and the precious coolant began to flow again. Gradually, the high-pitched jet roar of the overheating furnace began to drop to a steady hum.

But Gannon wasn't finished yet. For him, all that mattered was to eliminate Tia. Once that was done, he could easily put the cooling system out of action again. He grabbed Tony roughly by the arm. 'You've got to get her this time,' he growled. 'Levitate that transformer – and hit her with it!'

Accordingly, one of the huge 1,000-pound transformers that were stored at the base of the wall, began to rise slowly in the air. Then, like a VTOL jet, it suddenly flashed towards its target. Crusher yelped fearfully, but Tia stayed calm. Thinking quickly, she energized another of the transformers and sent it flying through the air on an interception course. Her timing was perfect and the two heavy missiles collided with a tremendous crash, disintegrating and raining a shower of fragments down on to the floor. Tia and Crusher dived for cover.

Gannon seethed. He had to find a way to stop this interfering young whelp. His eyes alighted on an untidy pile of metal piping. 'Tony,' he commanded, boiling with frustration, 'throw those metal pipes at her! And don't miss this time!'

Half a dozen of the long steel pipes raised themselves to shoulder-height. They hovered for a moment, then, like shafts loosed from a bow, swished away towards their target. Gannon gritted his teeth.

But Tia thwarted him again. At the last second, she energized a big metal cabinet and brought it across in front of her body, like a shield. The steel arrows thudded harmlessly home. Touché.

Gannon glanced upwards. He had heard shouts from above and now he could see the struggling figures of Letha, Sickle and the three boys up on the catwalk. His partners didn't appear to be doing any better than he was. Then he caught sight of the gantry crane and the idea came to him in a flash. Why hadn't it occurred to him before? 'Listen very carefully, Tony,' he said evenly. 'You will pretend to remember Tia. You will talk to her . . . lure her to the centre of the aisle.' His eyes flicked upwards. 'Then you will cause the crane to drop its cargo on her. Is that clear?' Tony nodded, quite impassive. 'Then go now,' prompted Gannon. 'Call to her . . .'

Tony stepped out into the aisle, where he knew Tia could see him. At first, his expression was as vacant as ever. Then, convulsively, he jerked a hand to his forehead and allowed a confused smile to spread across his face. He shook his head, as if trying to clear it. 'Tia . . .' he said unsteadily. He pronounced the name as though it were a foreign word.

Tia emerged cautiously from behind the battered cabinet. Her heart lifted. 'Tony . . .?' she questioned, hopefully.

Her brother took a few uncertain steps towards her. 'I . . . I'm starting to remember you . . . Tia . . .'

Tia couldn't believe her ears. Was Tony finally regaining his senses? She took another step forward. 'Your voice sounds so strange,' she said. 'What's wrong?'

'I don't know exactly but I need help.'

'You'll be all right now.'

'Tell her to come to you,' hissed Gannon into the control unit.

'Tia,' said Tony, stretching out his hand, 'get me out of here.'

Tia began walking towards her brother, stepping carefully through the debris of the smashed transformers. Her heart pounded madly.

'Stop there! Don't come any closer!' shouted Tony, arms raised in warning.

'Why not?' said Tia, coming to a standstill. The massive container hanging from the crane loomed over her.

'Er ... because of the radiation.'

'The radiation isn't a problem with us.' Tia received her first shudder of suspicion. Why was Tony being so illogical?·

'Drop it on her, Tony!' shouted Gannon, unable to contain his voice any longer.

Tia watched in horror as the square shadow in which she was standing shrank to a third of its size in the space of a heartbeat. Even before she looked up she felt a horrible rush of air on the back of her neck. With split seconds to spare, she energized the container and it came to a shuddering halt inches above her head.

Gannon leapt out from concealment. 'Tony,' he yelled, 'exert a force greater than hers! Crush her!'

Abruptly the weight of the container began to increase. The force of gravity and the power of Tony combined were too much for Tia. Slowly, agonizingly, she began to sink beneath the enormous weight. 'Tony, no ...' she pleaded. But her cries went unheeded. Pressed down to the floor, Tia called on every ounce of her mental strength to keep the container from squashing her into a pancake.

'Finish her!' demanded Gannon. 'Finish her.' He was obsessed with the thought of his imminent triumph. Too obsessed in fact, for his own good. As Tia lay there, fighting for her life, she realized for the first time what was keeping Tony's mind enslaved: it was the device Gannon held in his right hand. Instantly, she knew exactly what to do.

Gannon practically jumped out of his skin as Tia's diverted flow of energy spun the control unit out of his hand. It curved through the air, trailing a slipstream of bright red sparks and crash-landed on the floor in a puff of blue smoke. Gannon let out a frantic gasp and scrabbled to retrieve it.

Tia was off the hook. Without Tony's force behind it, the metal container presented no problem at all and Tia quickly levitated it back up to the crane. Crusher dashed across to help her to her feet. Recovering quickly she reached out and grabbed her brother who was wincing in pain and had both hands clamped over his right ear. 'Tony, look at me!' she demanded. He twisted his head from side to side. 'It hurts,' he cried.

Carefully, Tia prised Tony's hands away from his ear and found the tiny receptor almost immediately. She quickly removed it and flung it to the floor, crushing it underfoot. Instantly, Tony's pain ceased. 'Tia!' he exclaimed, bewildered. 'Where are we? What's happened?'

By way of reply, Tia reached forward and placed the palms of her hands either side of Tony's head. In this way, they achieved total telepathic communion. In the space of a few seconds, Tia updated Tony with all the events of the past five days: his capture; the raid on the museum; the chase; the crash; the trap at the laboratory; the fight in the furnace room. Every detail was instantly digested.

'I did all that?' asked Tony, amazed. 'And he made me do it?' he added, pointing to Gannon.

Tia nodded. They turned to look at the distraught Gannon as he scurried around after his control unit which was hopping and jumping like a firecracker. Eventually, he managed to grab it but not for long. Tony energized the unit and it blew apart in Gannon's hands, leaving him with a pile of ashes and a surprised – and very blackened – face. But he still didn't give up. 'Tony,' he begged, 'please ... it isn't too late! We can still make use of molecular control!'

Tony pretended to think about it for a moment. Finally he said, 'Okay, Doctor, let's do it!'

It wasn't quite what Gannon was expecting. His mouth sagged open as he began to rise straight up into the air. Held helpless in Tony's energizing grip, he was made to turn a series of spectacular twists and somersaults. Eventually, Tony sent him high up to the roof, and deposited him on a narrow wooden lifting platform. Gannon clutched fearfully at the thin supporting wires, trembling like a leaf. 'Help,' he croaked, in a barely audible voice. 'Help ...'

Right on cue, Letha emerged from the depths of the furnace room tugging Rocky and Muscles along by their ears. She stopped dead as she came face to face with the reunited Tia and Tony. She gulped, and taking a quick glance up towards the lifting platform, she produced a sickly grin and gently released her two captives. She gave them each an affectionate pat on the head. With the grin still glued in position, she said, 'Well, why don't we all go and have some candy and soda and cake and ... oh, oh ...'

Her voice trailed away as her feet left the ground and she glided up to join her partner on the platform. The two of them didn't have to wait long for their partner. A second later, Tia spotted Sickle cowering on the catwalk and sent him up to complete the haul. Back down on the floor, the Earthquakes gathered round to shake Tony's hand and welcome him back to reality. 'We wanna join your gang,' said Crusher eagerly.

'But I don't have a gang,' said Tony.

'You do now,' corrected Dazzler, and the Earthquakes nodded their agreement. Tia smiled. Tony was clearly a big hit with her friends. It was a pity they hadn't been able to meet earlier. She had the feeling that . . . Her train of thought came to a sudden stop. It had completely slipped her mind!

'Tony!' she said, grabbing her brother's hand. 'It's Friday!'

The sun was dipping low behind the city rooftops as the minibus came rattling into the empty parking lot and braked to a juddering halt. As everyone piled noisily out, Tia found time to have a quiet aside with her brother. 'It's my fault the minibus is such a mess,' she explained. 'And they'll never get it to work without us in it.'

Tony nodded. 'We'd better fix it,' he agreed. 'I'm sure it'll be okay with Uncle Bené. I'll do a motor job and you do the bodywork.'

With that, they both turned to concentrate on their respective tasks. Yoyo and the Earthquakes had seen them perform many amazing feats, but this one was rather special. Like a film being run in reverse, the minibus began to transform itself back into a new vehicle. Dents popped back into shape, torn metal welded together, scratches faded into the paintwork, and the engine overhauled itself. When it was finished, the minibus sparkled from radiator grill to exhaust pipe and the engine sang as sweetly as a bird.

Yoyo was stunned. 'What's going on? I don't understand ...!' he blustered.

Tony shrugged. 'Looks like the molecules have rearranged themselves,' he said lightly.

The deep lines at the side of Yoyo's mouth creased upwards. He was smiling, although his face still looked as mournful as ever. 'You know what this means?' he said. 'They never saw the wreck. I'll tell them reports were exaggerated ...' He looked appealingly at the Earthquakes. 'And if you kids would come back to school, especially after we averted that disaster ... I'm sure they won't fire me. You'll come back ... won't you?'

The Earthquakes lowered their heads and shuffled uneasily. They looked as if they had just found a dead fly in a plate of their favourite food. Finally, Muscles said hesitantly, 'If we go back to school ... could we get to be as smart as Tia and Tony?'

'Maybe even smarter,' prompted Tia.

There was a long awkward silence. Then Dazzler shrugged and said, 'Well, you guys ... let's give it a shot.'

The Earthquakes nodded reluctantly. If Tia was behind the idea, then it might just be worth doing. They didn't have to look happy about it, though.

'Great!' bubbled Yoyo. 'I only hope the school can take it.' Then he jumped happily back into his cab, eager to inspect his shining new minibus.

It was time for Tia and Tony to be on their way. With the Earthquakes tagging along, they made off towards the stadium at a brisk run. When they reached the main gates, Tia and Tony got everyone to line up and link hands. To squeals of delight, they levitated the whole group up and across to the other side. Running on through the concrete passageway they passed through the stadium and out on to the field.

The Earthquakes had come to expect anything where Tia and Tony were concerned, but the sight of a shining silver spacecraft hovering a few feet over the fifty-yard line was more than enough to make them gasp with surprise.

'Wow!' said Rocky. 'A flying saucer!'

'These kids have everything!' said Crusher, stupified.

'Will we ever see you again?' asked Muscles.

'It's hard to say,' said Tony.

They shook hands and said their goodbyes, and Tia leant forward to kiss each of the Earthquakes in turn. 'Thanks for letting me be in the gang,' she said, 'and don't cry. We may come back soon.'

'Aw,' said Dazzler, 'I'm only crying cause I don't wanna go back to school.'

Tia smiled and then she and her brother turned and walked off across the field towards their waiting craft. As they drew near it, the teleporter beam shot down to the ground, and Uncle Bené emerged to greet them. 'Where are your suitcases?' he asked.

'We lost them,' explained Tia. 'There were a few problems.'

Uncle Bené raised his eyebrows. 'But did you have a good time?'

'Terrible,' moaned Tony. 'I knew we should have gone surfing.' Uncle Bené looked puzzled, but he supposed he would get to hear the full story on their journey back to Witch Mountain. Stepping into the beam, the three of them were lifted up into the body of their craft.

At the edge of the field, the Earthquakes heard a

high-pitched whine and watched sadly as the saucer rose up into the sky and disappeared over the rim of the stadium. Turning, they raced back through the concrete passageway, clambered over the gates, and ran towards the parking lot.

The minibus was waiting for them with its engine ticking over. 'Hey, Yoyo ... er, I mean ... Mr Yokomoto,' said Muscles, pausing in the doorway, 'Tia and Tony just took off in a flying saucer!'

Yoyo shook his head in disbelief. 'I've seen those kids work miracles,' he said. 'I believe a lot of things ... but I don't believe that! Get in!'

The Earthquakes shrugged and piled in. Still shaking his head, Yoyo slipped into first gear and his beautiful new minibus purred softly away towards the edge of the parking lot. If he had bothered to look behind him, he might well have wondered why, a moment later, his passengers had their heads out of the rear windows and were waving frantically towards the sky.

Then again, even if he had seen the silver blur streaking across the darkening horizon towards the distant range of mountains, he would never have believed it.